easy for you

stories

Shannan Rouss

Simon & Schuster Paperbacks

New York   London   Toronto   Sydney

Simon & Schuster Paperbacks
A Division of Simon & Schuster, Inc.
1230 Avenue of the Americas
New York, NY 10020

First Simon & Schuster trade paperback edition April 2010

SIMON & SCHUSTER PAPERBACKS and colophon are registered
trademarks of Simon & Schuster, Inc.

For information about special discounts for bulk purchases,
please contact Simon & Schuster Special Sales at
1-866-506-1949 or business@simonandschuster.com.

The Simon & Schuster Speakers Bureau can bring authors
to your live event. For more information or to book an event,
contact the Simon & Schuster Speakers Bureau at
1-866-248-3049 or visit our website at www.simonspeakers.com.

Designed by Jacquelynne Hudson

Manufactured in the United States of America

10 9 8 7 6 5 4 3 2 1

Library of Congress Cataloging-in-Publication Data

Rouss, Shannan. Easy for you : stories / Shannan Rouss.
p.   cm.
1. Los Angeles (Calif.)—Fiction. 2. Short stories. I. Title.
PS3618.O8698E26 2010 8
13'.6—dc22   2009026701

ISBN 978-1-4391-4835-8
ISBN 978-1-4391-5260-7 (ebook)

For my grandmothers

Hearing your words, and not a word among them . . .

—EDNA ST. VINCENT MILLAY

contents

easy for you

die meant enough

This was the summer our cars overheated and everyone's air conditioner—if you were lucky enough to have an air conditioner—often gave up. It was the summer of brush fires and brownouts, when all of Los Angeles dimmed its lights, casting an amber glow that might have been pretty if it weren't so hot, so impossible to be in your own skin. It was the summer I swore off meat, not all meat, just beef, and not for any moral reason, but on account of all those cows, the ones going mad. And it was the summer, it will forever be the summer, I dated a married man. Married insofar as he had a wife, a soon-to-be ex-wife, but a wife all the same, along with a daughter and a home, two bedrooms by the beach.

A marriage can happen in an instant. Sign here, say "I do," kiss the bride. But a divorce, the careful disconnecting of two people, can take months, years even, depending on the circumstances. There is the trial separation followed by the real separation. Lawyers are hired and possessions divided, the couch, the DVDs, the dog—in Brian's case, a Tibetan terrier his wife trained in Hebrew. *Boy* meant "come" and *die* meant "enough."

Brian's divorce, so far, had been amicable. It was a "friendly" divorce. A hi-how-are-you divorce. He and his wife lived in the same house at different times, one week on, one week off. They did this for Naomi's sake. The child came first. Of course, the child came first. That summer, I would have settled for second or third. Even fourth.

Brian held up one of Naomi's paintings and asked me what I thought. He had put Naomi to bed, and it was just the two of us, Brian and me, unless you counted the dog sprawled on the living room floor and hogging the fan.

"It's nice," I said, studying the damp puddly image.

"Do you think it seems dark?" Brian asked. "Or angry?"

He was looking for a sign. We all were. A few days earlier, both my fortune cookie and my horoscope had told me to think with my head, not with my heart. My friends had been saying the same thing for a while now. Only in less aphoristic ways.

No one wishes for this. No one dreams of becoming someone's second wife. But if you're alone long enough, you're bound to be someone's second something no matter what. It had only taken me a few nights to become inured to sleeping in the same bed Brian's wife had slept in. In the mornings, I would peek into her closet and look through her drawers. I used her shampoo and lotion. I had never met her, but I felt connected to her. And not in an adversarial way. Eventually, months from now, years perhaps, I thought we might meet for coffee or drinks.

But Brian thought otherwise. He said she was difficult to like. She never got along with his friends or his family. She was abrasive and opinionated, quick to anger. He called her fiery. But this was what he had chosen. This was what he had been drawn to.

I had asked him why he married her.

"You were obviously in love with her at some point," I said.

He sighed, deeply sucking in as if dragging on a joint. He told me that his wife was different from the women he had dated in the past. She had grown up in Israel. She ate tomatoes as if they were apples and knew how to handle an Uzi. She was exotic and beautiful.

"I guess I valued the wrong things," he said, and I had nodded as if it were a consolation, the fact that exotic and beautiful were no longer as important to him.

There were pictures of her still on the refrigerator, images from over the years. She and I looked nothing alike, although we looked like two women who could have been friends, women who shopped at the same boutiques and liked the same restaurants. Her family was from North Africa—Morocco or Egypt—while I was Eastern European if you went back far enough, fair-skinned with limp blonde hair.

Last week, Brian's wife found a strand of my hair in the shower. This had given me some satisfaction, the fact that I mattered to her, that I was even on her radar. I liked to imagine her showing up for her week, searching the bookshelves and drawers, looking for clues, small changes to the way things might have been, trying to piece together the person I was.

Recently, I had started leaving things behind. It began with a magazine on the coffee table and a bottle of white wine in the refrigerator—innocuous items, more passive than aggressive.

When Brian and I had arrived at the house this week, I found the magazine in the bathroom, balanced on the tub's edge, warped and opened to some article about an actor's fourth wedding. This was reassuring. You could trust a woman who reads magazines in the bathroom. You could be friends with her. Good friends. As for the bottle of wine, it was half empty. Or half full, depending on who you were rooting for.

While Brian was in the kitchen getting us beers, I sat on the couch and removed my bra, pulling it through my sleeve in one quick motion. The bra was nude—or was it beige? It was a beige bra, a politically correct bra. It didn't discriminate. I stashed it between two cushions as Brian strode back into the room, proudly holding a drink in each hand. He was barefoot and shirtless, wearing a pair of shorts that hung low on his narrow waist.

He handed me a beer and we clinked bottles. Brian wasn't a typical dad, not a barbecuing, tie on Father's Day dad. In fact, I don't think I had ever seen him in a suit. He played Frisbee and the guitar. He smoked American Spirits and drank Belgian beer, the kind made by Trappist monks who had taken a vow of silence but could still brew alcohol.

That night, after we ran out of beer and things to talk about— his marriage, my last boyfriend, his favorite music, my favorite books—we had sex on the couch and then again in the bed. It was in the bed, with his chest against my back, the bready scent of beer still on his breath, that he whispered the name Dahlia in my ear. Just once and barely audible, but loud enough that I heard it, and now I could never unhear it. Brian almost never spoke her name. The rare times that he did, it sounded like an apology, as if her name alone, the singularity of it, was enough to offend me.

But when he called me Dahlia, I didn't bother to correct him. I wasn't offended, at least not in the way I thought I'd be of-fended. I felt a sense of calm more than dread. It confirmed what I had suspected. Dahlia was always with us. There were three people in the relationship. There would always be three, even after the divorce was final and Brian had her initials removed from his arm or changed into something new.

"Die," I said to the dog the next morning. *"Die!"*

We were locked in a game of tug-of-war with my bra. The dog hunkered down, redoubling his efforts. He growled a don't-fuck-with-me-growl.

"Fine," I said. He could keep the bra.

Today would be the hottest day on record since 1963. You could feel it as soon as you stepped outside, the way the atmosphere had thinned, leaving almost nothing to protect you from the sun. I held up a hand to shade my face as we stood alongside Brian's car.

"Say good-bye," he said to Naomi, who was strapped into her car seat. She shook her head emphatically.

"C'mon, Naomi. Can you say good-bye?"

"No," she screamed before going quiet and playing absent-mindedly with the Velcro strap on her shoe.

"It's okay," I said.

"Sorry," Brian said.

"No sweat." I smiled, wiping my brow dramatically.

"Cute." He put his hand on my hip and left it there.

Naomi turned her head in our direction, eyeing us skeptically, awaiting our next move. Brian glanced at her and then at me.

"Adios," he whispered in my ear, and then pulled away and saluted me. I saluted him back. Just following orders.

The heat can make you do strange, unthinkable things. I read about a woman whose car broke down somewhere in the middle of nowhere. She was on her way to one of the Palms. Palm Desert, Palm Spring, Palm Valley. When the police found her, she was lying only twenty yards from the road, naked and unconscious.

They say that if you don't get enough water, you start walking in circles, talking to yourself, digging at the earth until your fingers bleed. Eventually, you get so hot you rip your own clothes off just to cool down.

I sat in my car and watched as the neighbors staggered from their homes. Everyone looked damp and soggy, wilting. They opened their car doors and waited a few moments before getting in. From the frying pan into the fire.

I should mention that this particular day was Friday, the

day the guards changed, when Brian and I left and Dahlia arrived. We had taken out the trash and changed the sheets in the morning. That was my idea. Clean sheets. Do unto others.

Dahlia worked three days a week at Barneys, the department store, not Barney's Beanery, that sports bar on Santa Monica with karaoke on Tuesdays. Where she worked was on Wilshire, past Saks and past Neiman's, closer to Rodeo. She was a personal shopper or a private shopper. A hush-hush shopper. I worked in the service industry as well. I was an accountant. An accountant in Beverly Hills, an accountant to the stars, but an accountant nonetheless.

I pushed the driver's seat back as far as it would go and propped my bare feet against the steering wheel. My toes were white nubs with coral polish on the nails. Coral was supposed to be in. The color was Conquistadorable.

I slipped my sweaty feet back in the canvas sneakers I had been wearing and continued to wait. Every twenty minutes or so, I pulled my car forward, moving as the shade did. I was under a thick, full-grown magnolia tree. Brian said it was more than two hundred years old. I never thought anything in Los Angeles, not anything that was still standing at least, had been around that long.

It was close to noon when Dahlia's car finally pulled into the driveway. I watched as she got out and tied her hair into a knot. She was like an apparition, all makeup-less and ethereal in her gauzy white sundress as the heat rose from the black driveway and hovered around her.

I got out of my car and walked toward her, smiling broadly and waving.

"Hi," I said.

"Hi," she said, studying my face for a moment. "Do we know each other?"

"I'm the woman," I said. "The 'other' woman," I added for

clarification, nervously making little quote signs with my fingers.

Dahlia looked at me and smiled. "So, you're my husband's girlfriend?" she asked. Her voice was raspy and hard like a smoker's, accent faint, although still there, lingering in the spaces between her words.

"Something like that," I said. Brian and I had been dating a few months and I wasn't sure what we were yet. He certainly never referred to me as his girlfriend. He hadn't even bothered to ask if I was seeing anyone else.

"You're in love?" she said.

"It's still early." I licked the sweat off my upper lip and swallowed.

"So maybe yes?"

I laughed. "I don't know."

She nodded, appraising me carefully.

"I just thought it would be a good idea for us to meet. You and me," I said, gesturing between the two of us as if there might be some confusion.

"Why?" She raised her dark eyebrows and waited.

"I thought it might make things easier."

"For who?"

"Everyone?"

She laughed and reached for something in her purse. "Smoke?" she said, taking out a pack of cigarettes.

"No."

"Of course not." She took her time lighting her cigarette and enjoyed her first few drags before speaking.

"It must be difficult," I said. I was trying to find some common ground, to get her to see how we were in this together.

"Difficult?"

"I mean the back-and-forth. The limboness of it all."

"Are you a therapist or something?" She was pointing at me with her cigarette.

I told her I was in therapy. But who wasn't? This was Los Angeles in the late nineties, when everyone was on Lexapro or Prozac or Zoloft, when even our therapists had therapists.

"My therapist didn't tell me to do this," I said.

"Congratulations," she said. "You think for yourself."

"Brian doesn't even know," I added, hoping this confidence would somehow win her over.

She laughed. "Brian doesn't know a lot of things. He doesn't want to know. Do you understand what I mean? He is like this," she said, putting her hands on either side of her eyes and looking around.

"Tunnel vision?" I said, as if this were a game of charades.

She shook her head.

"Blinders?"

"Yes!" she said. "Blinders."

I wondered if I should stick up for Brian, if I should defend him to his soon-to-be ex-wife, but I wasn't sure whose side I was on. I wasn't sure whose side I wanted to be on. Brian believed in moving forward. He believed in cutting losses. He and I were different that way.

"Have you ever been married?" Dahlia asked.

I shook my head. I had been engaged once, but that was years ago. We were supposed to get married in Jamaica. He had a wife and two kids now. I had been invited to the wedding.

"I will never get married again," she said. "Marriage is for quitters." She laughed at her own joke.

I didn't know what to say next. Inside the house, the dog had started barking and Dahlia said something to it in Hebrew, something that sounded not so different from "shut up."

"Do you think you'll go back to Israel?" I asked her. Brian had said it was a possibility.

"Why? Would you like me to? It would be easier for you, no?" she said. "You could move in. You could have my life. All of it. Here, it's yours."

She stepped aside and swept her arm out and I simply stood there. I was stuck. I felt like I had been called on in school and couldn't come up with the right answer. And I had studied.

"What?" she said. "Now you don't want it?"

She tossed her keys in my direction. They hit my stomach and fell at my feet, landing on the parched grass.

"This is your chance," she said.

"I don't want to fight," I said, kicking the keys toward her.

"Who's fighting?" she said, looking around. "We're not fighting. We're talking. This is a conversation. A *negotiation*. I offer you my life, and I get—what? Tell me. What do I get?"

I looked at Dahlia and thought this would be an ideal time to faint, if fainting was something you could wish for. But hot as I was, my knees did not buckle, and my mind did not go blank. So I did the only thing left to do. I called her bluff. She said nothing as I bent down to pick up the keys. I fumbled with them at the door.

"It's the gold one," she said.

The dog was not happy to see me. He barked and eyed me with a look of contempt, although he kept his distance. The house was warm and smelled of diapers and mildew and old coffee. Brian had put Naomi's painting on the refrigerator. The photos of Dahlia were still there, including one that must have been taken in the hospital after Naomi was born. Dahlia was lying in a bed with a baby in her arms. It was the photo I had always liked best of her. She looks exhausted and vulnerable and kind.

I tried to get closer to the refrigerator but the dog was in the way, guarding his turf. He wasn't a big dog, but he was mean. I could see his black gums and sharp little teeth. Still, I managed to get close enough to grab the photo and slip it in my pocket. Then I turned around and left the house.

Dahlia was where I had left her. She pulled out her cigarettes and took one for herself, tapping it against the pack and then

holding it out toward me. This time, I took one. My hand trem-
bled as I held the cigarette to my lips, and Dahlia brought the
flame of her lighter towards me. It was the first time I had had
a cigarette sober in years. I gave Dahlia her keys and she smiled,
taking a step back to look me over.

"Well, you're not a complete idiot," she said.

I inhaled and hoped she was right.

swans by the hour

Alena is out on the deck, a magazine balanced in her lap, as she raises her firm brown legs up and down, engaging her stomach muscles. I watch as her abdomen twitches and shudders beneath her oiled skin. Alena is twenty-three, although she doesn't seem twenty-three. Or maybe it's that I don't seem thirty-eight, not the way my parents had seemed thirty-eight when they were my age. I tell dick jokes and do tequila shots. If she's hot. I send text messages (sometimes with emoticons) and call my friends by their last names.

Of course, I can pass for an adult. I'm boyish and balding, not prematurely, but right on time. I have a degree in computer science and a subscription to the *Wall Street Journal*. I sold a start-up and bought a house in Malibu, an Italian villa with postmodern influences, fully furnished, all the way down to the books. Even the picture frames on the piano were here when I arrived. The house is four-thousand-plus square feet of never-before-lived-in space. I've got one game room, three bedrooms, and four bathrooms, each with a TV. I could use one bathroom just for shitting, another for showering, and still have two left over. On weekends, I host dinner parties and pool parties. I serve wine and martinis and get everyone drunk. Here, have another. And another. And another.

People pass out in the guest rooms and on the couches. In the morning, I make cappuccinos with my integrated espresso machine, and we all try to piece together the details of what happened the night before: who fell into the pool first, which team won at charades, why we decided to open that last bottle of wine.

Over the years, I have come to realize that it's easier to commit to a house than a woman. I don't say this as some sort of epiphany, although okay, yes, it was for me. I love my house. My friends love my house. My friends love me for my house. Hell, I even love me for my house on some days. Everyone should know a person with a place like this, somewhere to watch the Super Bowl or celebrate on New Year's. But tomorrow night. This will be a first. My ex—one of my exes—is getting married here. In the backyard. It was bound to happen sooner or later with the sunset and the views and the pool. This is a house that deserves a wedding, something small and intimate, the kind of wedding you'd have if it was a second marriage. Or a third.

The ex and I dated for about five months, the point in relationships when women begin to shave less and expect more. That was three years ago. We've stayed friendly. We give each other rides to the airport and make sure to call on holidays and birthdays. We had sex once after we had broken up. We were both still single. And drunk. I told her I loved her, not something I had said when we were together. I think I even said it twice. But I was saying a lot of things, the usual fare. You're so sexy. I love your body. I'm gonna come so hard. Maybe she missed it—she never brought it up.

The ex—her name is Stacey—has been getting her PhD in Victorian literature for as long as I've known her. She has a thing for Jane Eyre the way other women have a thing for Angelina Jolie. Jane Eyre, she has said, is her girl crush, the woman she'd fuck if she fucked women. This is why we'd have never worked.

16

Tonight is the rehearsal dinner, although there's no actual rehearsal. What's there to rehearse? You walk down the aisle, you say I do. I will be attending alone because Alena is on the list somewhere else, somewhere more exclusive. Out by the pool, she's done with her stomach exercises and is smoking a cigarette. It's a nasty habit. A couple months ago, I hired an addiction coach for her. He was written up in a magazine. Kick butt. That was his motto. He forced her to smoke nonstop, one cigarette after the next. For four days straight. After that, she was supposed to never want to smoke again. Reverse psychology.

It didn't work. There were never any guarantees. Alena is stubborn. She came here from Slovakia about two years ago with the usual aspirations of being an actress. That's mostly who I date. Wannabe actresses or has-been models.

To Alena's credit, she was in two movies, cast once as "Beautiful Girl," and then as "Sorority Girl." In both movies, she ended up dead. That's the way it goes.

But right now, Alena is alive. Very much alive in her little black bikini and aviator sunglasses. She comes inside and brushes by me. I keep the thermostat set at a crisp sixty-seven degrees and her skin glistens with goose bumps.

"What are you looking for?" I ask. She makes herself at home, peering through items in my refrigerator.

"Iced tea."

"Third shelf, behind the cottage cheese."

She pours herself a glass and tells me it tastes like dirty water.

"So don't drink it."

"I have a sweet mouth," she says, fucking up the idiom. Or maybe just reinventing it. She starts opening cupboards and shutting drawers, making as much noise as possible.

"I'm working," I say.

She walks over to where I'm sitting and reads the nearly illegible notes I've made on a yellow legal pad.

"Stacey has not been known for her taste in men," she whispers. "Pause Laughter."

"It's not done."

"Your speech?"

I nod and tap my pen against the page.

"You want to practice? Go ahead. I'll be Stacey."

Alena walks around to the other side of the table and sits across from me. She rests her sharp chin on her fists and bats her eyes. People tell her she looks like Audrey Hepburn, only sturdier, with more meat and muscle on her tanned body.

She puts on a nasal American accent and says, "Hello, it's my wedding. I'm getting married in my ex-boyfriend's backyard. I'm so cool. I'm so progressed."

"Progressive," I say.

"Progressive."

I rip the speech off the pad and toss the page at Alena. "You're hilarious." I don't need these notes; I know the routine, the same tired jokes, references to past incidents, embarrassing stories. And then something about luck or fate, and happily ever after. Mazel tov. Drink.

I have nothing against marriage. I understand the evolutionary necessity of it. My parents have been together for forty-five years, and sure, they want grandkids, but right now they'll settle for cruises to Alaska and Mexico. It's not that I'm afraid of commitment. In fact, I'm a serial monogamist, although when I tell this to the women I date, they're not impressed. The fact that I've never been married is a strike against me. It makes me suspect.

But not with Alena. She is just vain enough to believe that I've been alone all these years because I never met anyone as perfect as her. This gives her hope.

She and I shower together before the rehearsal dinner, making me late, which I don't doubt was part of her plan. Alena has only seen a picture of Stacey. "She's pretty," she said, but I could tell from her tone that what she really meant was, "I'm prettier."

The dinner is at the Mexican restaurant where the waiters sing the menu. When Stacey sees me, she kisses the tips of her fingers and waves. Not one for convention, she's wearing a black dress. The fabric is flimsy like gauze. She appears infinitely fuckable, probably due in no small part to the fact she's off-limits. Verboten. Aren't men hardwired that way? We want what we can't have. Or maybe it's because she has lost weight. Not that she was ever fat, but there's something more elegant about her now. She told me she's been subsisting on almonds and egg whites and wine for the past week. It seems like the kind of diet that could make you live forever. Or die right away.

Stacey's fiancé, Sean, comes over to say hello. He's from New England and defiantly pasty. He teaches poetry to undergraduate students at UCLA, where Stacey is getting her PhD. Still.

"Good to see you," he says, patting me on the back. "I have someone for you to meet."

He keeps his hand on my shoulder and steers me over to a woman standing alone with a glass of wine. She makes a big show of sipping it, moving it around in her mouth, then swallowing.

"Joyce introduced me and Stacey," he says.

Joyce nods dramatically, as if confirmation is necessary.

"Is that so?" I say.

She swallows and then says, "They have such similar energies."

Sean pats us both on the shoulder, seemingly proud of the work he has done here, and says "Talk amongst yourselves" before casually striding away.

I attempt to make conversation, but Stacey is a distraction. Her skin is so white it glows. Maybe this is what Joyce meant by energies. Don't get me wrong. I don't want to date Stacey, much less marry her. I want her to be happy. Is it possible to feel pater-nal toward someone and still want to ravage her? God I hope not.

"Do you practice yoga?" Joyce asks me.

I tell her I've tried power yoga and she smiles sympatheti-cally.

"I'm a student of Ashtanga," she says.

"That's great." I'm a student of bullshit.

"It's about movement and breath." She closes her eyes and in-hales.

"Do you need another drink?"

She holds up her glass for inspection. It is nearly empty. "White wine," she says. "Thank you."

"*Namaste*," I say backing away, grateful for the escape.

"*Namaste*," she says.

The atmosphere during dinner is appropriately festive and nostalgic. Someone, probably Stacey's mother, has provided sombreros and maracas, not enough for everyone, but the guests are generous. They pass the accoutrements around, taking turns posing in full regalia. It's Stacey's sister who finally stands up and shakes the maracas, trying to get everyone's attention. When that fails, she yells, "Hey, everybody. It's my turn." She's older than Stacey by a couple years and has never been married. She's the less attractive version of Stacey, a test run, the beta model.

She wears a sombrero and it keeps sliding down on her small head. She shakes the maracas one more time for good measure and swings her hips, attempting to be seductive. The crowd finally quiets and she begins.

"Okay, I have to give the requisite speech tomorrow, so to-night I will keep it short and sweet. Stacey, you have been an amazing older sister." She winks and waits for people to get the joke. There are a few courtesy chuckles.

"Seriously," she says, "you may be the little sister, but I've al-ways looked up to you. For those of you who don't know, Stacey is smarter, funnier, and probably nicer than me. And now she's more married than me."

People smile uncomfortably and Stacey's sister pushes the sombrero up so she can read the note cards she's holding. God, this girl is breaking my heart. I feel like I should get down on one knee and propose to her just to put an end to this.

"Seriously," she says again. "I'm really happy for you two. You give me hope. So that's good," she continues, speaking more slowly now, really taking her time. Someone has the good sense to shout "l'chaim," and we all drink and clap and sit through another half hour of old-fashioned toasting and roasting. A single maraca is passed around like a conch—only he who has it may speak. The woman beside me forgoes her turn and suddenly it's in my hands.

"Is this thing on?" I say, hitting the top of the maraca. I'm doing my Catskills schtick, warming up the crowd.

"Wait, wait, wait," Stacey interrupts. She stands up. "For those of you who don't know, this is my dear friend who has so generously offered his home to Sean and me, which is where we'll be getting married tomorrow."

People clap and I feel like a jackass. Dear friend, eh? I wonder how Sean feels, having his wedding in the backyard of a man who used to sleep with his fiancée. Then again, Sean was married once before. That must put everything in perspective.

"What Stacey doesn't know," I say, "is that she's getting the bill next week."

Everyone laughs heartily.

"Stacey," I say. "In the past, your taste in men has been questionable. At best." I pause briefly and steal a sip of tequila while the crowd waits, their heads tilted attentively toward me.

"But now," I continue, "you have officially redeemed yourself."

Stacey smiles and blows me another little kiss like she did when I arrived. Was she always this coy? I don't remember her being a kiss blower, but there's something about the gesture that suits her, or suits us. It's like a stage whisper, a secret out in the open.

"You know," I say, taking another gulp of my drink and hitting my stride. "They say that you don't know what you've got until it's gone. And I'm inclined to believe that."

The room is quiet. The guests look at me, waiting for what's next. So I keep going.

"Here's the thing, folks, when I was with Stacey, I didn't appreciate her. I didn't hold her dear. And she deserves to be held dear. We all do."

I turn to Sean and speak directly to him. "You hold that girl dear," I say. "You know what I mean? She can be difficult—sorry, Stacey," I say, nodding at her, "but yeah, you can be."

She smiles and I take this as a sign of encouragement. "She's impatient," I say to the crowd, and then again look to Stacey. Sean puts his arm around her.

"You are, my love. And you interrupt. I can't get through a sentence without her asking some inane question. You cheat at Scrabble and you talk with your mouth full. And you don't take criticism well."

Stacey is just staring at me expectantly, the smile still on her face, waiting for the punch line. Someone boos.

"Right. Let me try again," I say. "What I mean is that, Sean, you've got to hold her dear because of all these things, not in spite of them. I just wish someone had told me that. Come to think of it, someone probably did tell me that. So, okay, cheers, best wishes, be well, et cetera, et cetera."

It's Joyce who first approaches me after the maraca is retired. "That was some speech," she says.

In the morning, memories of the night before come back in blurry, unfortunate thuds as my mind sloshes about. I seem to recall Sean and I having the kind of conversation that ends with a hug. We were overly earnest. Liquor and special occasions will do that to you. As for Stacey, she avoided me. Or maybe I avoided her. Either way, we never spoke. Perhaps wisely so. I see on my phone that I called Alena at 11:28. Gratefully, she didn't answer.

It's the day of the wedding and I have woken up in the same clothes I wore last night, so I change into a more respectable T-shirt and sweatpants. When I get downstairs, there are strangers dressed all in white and moving efficiently around my kitchen like nurses in triage. They fold napkins into complex origami flowers and count silverware, separating the salad forks from the dinner forks, the soupspoons from the teaspoons.

"Good morning," I say. A few of them glance up and nod in my direction before resuming their tasks.

"Cereal," I say, as if I need a reason to be in here. I get out some kind of cholesterol-lowering, shit-inducing, age-fighting cereal. When I open my refrigerator, where one would expect to find milk, there is no milk. Only white trays stacked one on top of the next. The hors d'oeuvres. Hors devors. Horse divorce.

"Here," a woman says. She hands me a flute of champagne and I take it.

"Breakfast of champions," I say, and wander into the living room. The floors in here, I have been told, are from Italy. The tiles are one of a kind. Handmade. Baked in the Tuscan sun.

The champagne goes down smoothly and when I finish the glass, I return to the kitchen for more. The woman who poured the glass the first time is indiscernible from the rest of the workers, all with their hair tied back and their heads down. So I help myself.

"Just getting some bubbly," I say when someone looks over her shoulder at me. "A little bubbly. Bubbly, bubbly, bubbly."

She nods. Maybe she thinks I'm drunk. Maybe I still am. The stupor hasn't fully worn off yet. I lie down on the couch, and my live-in Franzia trudges down the stairs. She has her purse on her shoulder and her keys in her hand. I have given her the day off.

"You okay?" she asks. "You need something before I go?"

"Where are you going?" I don't want to be alone.

"To see my daughter and her kids."

"You have a daughter?" I say.

"Shush." Franzia has been with me for the past year. She knows I know about her daughter, the one who lives in Sylmar, in the earthquake hot zone where houses are the first to crumble.

Franzia is standing above me. I reach a hand up and she takes it.

"Yes?" she says. Her hand is warm and dry as wood.

"Maybe we should get married," I say. We practically are already. We live together, she cleans, I pay the bills, we never have sex.

"You got it," she says. Franzia is a widow. Her husband used to pave the freeways.

"I love you, Franzia," I say.

She laughs. "Okay. See you tomorrow."

I don't know how long I'm on the couch, but when I open my eyes again, there are flowers and tablecloths and chairs, all white as soap, and I hear someone say, "Where do you want the geese?"

"Swans. I ordered swans," Stacey's mother says. She is wearing jeans and running shoes and a baseball hat that says "Mother of the Bride."

"Did we wake you?" she asks when I sit up.

"No, no. Make yourself at home."

"That's what I meant," the man with the gaggle says. "Where do you want the swans?"

The swans stand in the entryway, their beady black eyes darting nervously around the house. They look at one another and cock their heads to the side, as if weighing their options, perhaps considering an escape route.

It's agreed that the birds should go in the pool. The man as-sures us that their wings are clipped, so they will hang out there until he comes back to retrieve them.

Stacey's mother identifies everything as successful or unsuc-cessful: haircuts, vacations, meals. And now the centerpieces are successful, as are the swans. She tells me she's renting them by the hour. "They're a surprise," she adds.

I nod. They certainly are. Everything so far has been a sur-prise.

Back when Stacey had asked to have the wedding here, she prefaced it by saying I could say no. She would understand. But that would mean there was something to understand, something to say no to. So I said yes.

With this house, I thee wed.

I look at Stacey's mother. Her arms are soft and dimpled. Her hair is dyed blonde and she's wearing bright pink lipstick. There are only maybe fifteen years between us tops, but it's fifteen years in the wrong direction.

"When's it going to be your turn, mister?" she asks.

"Depends on how long Stacey and Sean last." I wink at her and she looks perplexed, like she is replaying the line in her head to figure out whether or not it was funny.

"If you want to be helpful," she says, her tone more serious now, "we need to put lights along the railing."

I don't particularly want to be helpful. "Let me get dressed," I say.

Upstairs in my room, I call Alena. This is what I love about her, that she is not a part of the world I am in right now. She doesn't fit in here; she is too young and carefree for all this. I listen to her voice mail recording, which is stern but sexy: "You have reached the phone of Alena Lubas. Please leave your number even if you believe I already have it." After a pause, she says, "I will return your call at my earliest convenience."

I don't bother to leave a message. Instead I try to jerk off, but there are bagpipes outside, loud and whiny. Waah, waah, waah. Someone warming up for the processional. Sean is getting married in a skirt. He's half Scottish. That will make Stacey's kids one quarter Scottish. Her sons could one day get married in skirts too. They could one day get married in my backyard. They may even call me uncle and I'll leave them a little something in my will.

Someone knocks at my door.

"Come in," I sing, my bottom half naked under the covers. I lie in bed like an invalid taking visitors.

"We have a crisis," Stacey's mother says. She has her cell phone in one hand, ready for action.

My first thought is that the swans are making a run for it. They may not be able to fly, but they're no dummies.

"The groom's cake is in Santa Barbara," she says. "Practically Santa Barbara. By the outlet mall in Oxnard. Flat tire."

"The cake has a flat tire?" I say, trying to be funny. But this is apparently not a time to be funny.

"It's dairy-free," she says. Because Sean's stomach can't handle the milk, she explains, and this bakery, the one in Santa Barbara, was written up in *Martha Stewart Living*. Well, fuck me in the ass, why didn't someone say so?

So now I'm expected to rescue the special-ordered cake, which probably tastes like wet newspaper with shit for frosting. As if one cake isn't enough.

"I know it would mean a lot to Stacey," her mother says, adding that she will reimburse me for gas.

"I'll add it to the bill," I say, and she laughs nervously, then tells me I'm a lifesaver.

"This is a mitzvah," she says, looking up toward the ceiling, where God no doubt resides.

I don't do the mitzvah, but ours is a merciful God and I decide that he—or she!—will forgive me. Of course, I don't know if

Stacey's mother ever will. By four o'clock, I have three messages from her. The last one says, "I'm starting to worry now. Should I call the police?"

She shouldn't call the police. I have checked into the Sunset Marquis. I didn't disregard the cake to be an asshole, although yes, it may have been an assholey thing to do. But when I got in the car, Alena had called.

"I'm coming over," she said. Of course, there was nowhere to come over to, so I picked her up at her place in West Hollywood and we went straight to the hotel. The place is small and unassuming, tucked away at the end of a dead-end street. It's got private bungalows and a checkered past.

Alena and I are lying in bed and I'm busy running my fingers through her hair, which smells like apples.

"Do you want to get married?" I say.

She looks up at me with her mouth slightly open, her front teeth resting on her lip. She has an overbite that's charming even though it inhibits her ability to give expert head. "To you?"

"Sure," I say.

She bites my nipple a little too hard and sits up. "Please," she says, rolling her eyes. "You need to give me a ring. I wasn't born yesterday." How she loves her American idioms.

"I have to pee," she says. I watch as she walks to the bathroom on her tiptoes. There is a constellation of zits on her ass and I'm not even bothered by them. That has to count for something.

After we finish all the liquor in the minibar, Alena opens the cashews. Nine dollars for the jar. Twenty-five cents a nut. She's worth it.

I look at the time on my phone. It's almost seven o'clock. By now, complete strangers have probably shit in my bathrooms and gone through the pills in my medicine cabinets. Concern for the cake—and for me, I suppose—seems to have subsided; there are no more messages from Stacey's mother.

"Where are they going on their honeymoon?" Alena asks me.

She is sucking the salt off the cashews and spitting them into her palm. Too many calories, she tells me.

"Uganda, I think." Or maybe it was Botswana.

"Why?" she asks, letting a nut fall from her mouth.

"It makes them interesting."

"It makes them stupid." Alena says she wants to go to Hawaii or Anguilla for her honeymoon. I didn't even know she had ever heard of Anguilla.

"I saw it on the *Today* show," she explains.

"Let's go," I say.

"To Anguilla?"

"To dinner."

Staying in a hotel a couple miles from where you live will make the world feel different to you, as if you're taking a vacation from your own life, right as it's happening. It will make you existential and philosophical, which is how I feel right now, like I'm supposed to do something drastic. So while Alena is in the shower singing "Material Girl"—at least the words she knows— I reach past her slimy pile of cashews and grab a pad of paper.

"Forgot something at me casa," I write. "Order room service. Sky's the limit."

Because of the glut of cars, I'm forced to park up the road in front of a neighbor's house. Sensor lights go on and a dog barks as I get out of the car. I wave in the general direction of the house just so that no one thinks I'm doing anything suspicious.

As I walk into my own house, faces I've never seen before greet me, men in kilts smoking a joint in my front yard. They nod and say what's up and pretend like we're all old friends. I go along with it. This is a party, after all.

Once I'm secure in my bedroom, I have a safe view of the party. The lights have successfully been strung along the railing. I can't find Stacey in the crowd of pale, fluttery dresses. Isn't there supposed to be some rule against this—women wearing the same shade as the bride?

I look beyond the party to the beach. It is empty and dark, not black, but blue like the moon. It's terrifying, the vastness of it. I think of my parents and their cruises. I don't know how they manage it, all that open space with no end in sight.

I open the door and step out onto the balcony, where I yell Stacey's name. I'm tempted to add, "Wherefore art thou?" No one can hear me anyway—the DJ is playing that song, the one about Jack and Diane and the heartland and doing the best they can. Everybody is clapping and singing along, and no one hears me, except for a swan that cocks its head in my direction. He's looking up at me as if I'm some kind of a bastard for disturbing the idyllic scene below. He's only doing his job.

Again, I yell Stacey's name, this time louder, and someone taps her shoulder. She has on a long white dress and flowers in her hair. She turns to me and I'm fairly certain she mouths "What the fuck?" like a pissed-off little wood nymph.

"Mea culpa," I yell, although I'm not quite sure what I'm apologizing for: failing to rescue the dairy-free groom's cake or being absent altogether. Or something entirely different. I look at Stacey and find myself thinking of Alena, counting her virtues. The reverse is also true—when I look at Alena I think of Stacey. It makes sense. We are a consumer culture. We comparative shop.

I get in bed, which seems like my best option. I am alone with my things, my possessions, all chosen by someone else like an arranged marriage, the best kind of marriage, perhaps, if you care to believe the statistics.

The music outside has stopped and the microphone squeals. The idiot is too close to the speakers. I was in a band in college. I know the drill. I hear Sean's voice as he apologizes for the technical difficulties and then begins his requisite gushing. He says something about being the happiest man alive. I have an urge to run downstairs and ask if he's telling the truth.

There is a hierarchy in the room.

The frailest, the ones who are all skin and bone and strappy tendons, are the most revered. By everyone. Even the doctors. They are women who do not bleed. They are hardly women at all with their hipless boy bodies and deflated breasts.

Then there are the women like me. Thin, but not thin enough. We can pass for normal, elude detection. However during meals, if you watch carefully, if you know what to look for, you will see the way our eyes dart across the table, like animals scavenging for food. We keep track of who ate what and how much, who left what behind. We can't imagine leaving anything behind. We are all or nothing. Feast or famine. When nobody is looking, we sneak a small bite, and another, and another, until our futile efforts at restraint are abandoned. We give into our desires and then punish ourselves for it.

There is one woman, a wildcard, who eats paper. No one knows what to make of her. She says envelopes are her weak spot.

Finally, there are the women who are always exposed, all their soft, white fleshiness impossible to hide. Even the dresses like tents cannot hide them, so they avert their eyes. They pretend to study their unwrinkled hands, the skin stretched taut, or their wide feet squeezed into shoes they have to buy at specialty stores. Their arms are bigger, many times bigger, than the spindly legs of the women in the first group. They can't imagine that under all the fat, they too are bones.

There are ten of us altogether, enough for a minyan, enough for us to pray. The doctors here believe we can all learn from one another. They have a theory: that the reason behind the problem is the same for all of us, that it just manifests itself in different ways.

I have my own theory. I think that the overeaters wish they could be bulimic. That, if nothing else, they had the nerve to stick their fat fingers down their throats. And I think that the bulimics wish they could be anorexic, that they could get by on water and lettuce alone, and I think that the anorexics have no intention of getting better. What could be better than this?

Ben brought me here three weeks ago. Ben is a chef. A bulimic dating a chef. It feels like it has to mean something, to be part of some bigger plan. Or a bad movie. Ben thinks food is sacred. He speaks of it in hushed and reverent tones, waxing poetic about heirloom tomatoes and fontina cheese and semolina bread. Once I am better, Ben promises that we will take a trip to Italy. We will have truffles in Piedmont, pizza in Sicily, and gelato in Rome. Italy is our goal. Italy is our test.

I listen, or half listen, as our group leader, Lori S., says the usual pyschobabble about loving ourselves. Lori S. is frail yet maternal despite her sharp corners. She is almost as skinny as the anorexics—she used to be one herself. And being an anorexic is something like being an alcoholic. The disease gets you for life. Of course, Lori S. tells us she's living with an eating disorder, not dying with one. Every day is a battle. Every day she has to choose her life. Her health. Blah, blah, blah. I'd like nothing more than to give her a goddamn candy bar and see if she chooses that.

"What do you think?" she asks me.

"What do I think about what?"

"Do you remember the last time you loved yourself?"

This sounds like a question about masturbation, although I'm pretty sure it's not. I'm pretty sure that's a different meeting altogether.

"Not really," I say. I remember hating my thighs at seven. I remember getting on the scale at eight and hoping I would never weigh more than the sixty pounds I was then. I remember the day my mother's clothes became too small for me to dress up in.

"Come on," Lori S. says, as if all I need is a little goading.

"Where are we going?" I say.

"You have a disease," one of the anorexics chimes in, a pained expression on her skeleton face. She doesn't merely starve herself. She works out too, which only makes the rest of us eating women feel twice as terrible about ourselves.

"Maybe you should think of it as like having cancer. Or something," she says.

"Or something," I say.

"I'm just trying to help. I thought you should be mindful."

You can tell which women have been here the longest, the veterans who speak the doctors' language. They are always talking about mindfulness, about checking in with yourself. Be mindful. Check in. The way they repeat these phrases, you'd think it was that simple.

I call Ben when group is over.

"How's it going?" he asks.

I know that what he really wants to ask me is if I'm still

tossing my cookies. Or praying to the porcelain god. Or selling Buicks. That one has always been my favorite.

"It's going," I say, which means I haven't sold a Buick in four days. "I think I'm ready for Italy. Or close to ready."

"How close?"

"Pasta close."

"You ate pasta?"

"Macaroni," I tell him, trying to manage his expectations. "Macaroni and low-fat cheese."

"How was it?" he asks.

Dear, sweet Ben, who always wants to know how the food was, who doesn't understand that that's not the point, that for me, that will never be the point.

"I got a high five," I say.

"Go team!"

"Exactly."

"When you come home, I'm going to make you real pasta. Vermicelli. Fresh tomatoes. Basil. Extra-virgin olive oil." He makes the clipped sound of a kiss.

A few days later, my three-week stint at the center in Malibu, camp for the gastronomically challenged, has come to an end. I have been healed. Praise Jesus. It's a little like graduating from nursery school. Like who the hell cares.

The doctors give me a journal as a parting gift. Thanks for playing. They urge me to remember my goals, to avoid triggers, to check in with myself and be mindful. I exchange phone numbers and e-mails with the other women and make false promises to keep in touch, as if we have anything in common besides food, or a lack thereof.

The anorexics, but mostly the overeaters, hug me. I try to wrap my arms all the way around their bodies. I add up the calories I burn with each hug.

When Ben arrives, he holds out a bouquet of pink balloons.

"What are these for?" I ask.

"Congratulations," he says, shrugging his shoulders. Congratulations are for getting a promotion or becoming engaged. I take the balloons anyway.

"You look great," he says. "Healthy." We hug awkwardly, pushing the balloons aside, wondering when to pull away, neither of us wanting to go first.

During the car ride home, I stare at the beach. We pass one facility after the next, hidden behind gates covered with lush foliage. It's Rehab Row, each place with a name more schmaltzy than the next: Promises, Passages, Harmony Place.

"Tired?" Ben asks.

"Not really."

"Music?"

"Sure."

He turns on the radio. It's the Allman Brothers' "Melissa." Ben keeps the beat on the steering wheel, hitting it with the tips of his fingers.

"Sweet Melissa," he croons, and then mumbles the rest of the lyrics.

When the song ends, he is out of breath. Ben wheezes when he overexerts himself. He keeps a syringe of epinephrine in his pocket.

"So about Italy?" he manages to gasp before reaching for his inhaler. He is testing the waters. He hopes that I'm cured, that having an eating disorder is like having the flu. He thinks it's that easy. If he didn't, he probably wouldn't still be here.

"About Italy," I say.

"I was thinking we could go in September."

"September is good."

The pink balloons are in the backseat, bobbling around on curled ribbons. I wonder how Ben can drive with them back there. I want to pop each one, hear the pleasantly startling snap of rubber bursting. I acknowledge this thought. I am mindful of it. But I don't act on it. Instead, I will let the balloons die their own slow death, deflating and sinking, becoming wizened little scraps.

Ben wants me to stay with him, at least until we go to Italy— the trip is only a few weeks away. I am in between jobs and in between apartments. In between everything, it seems. My only other option would be to stay at my mother's in Studio City. What used to be my childhood bedroom now doubles as a workout room. There is a recumbent bike in the corner and a collapsible StairMaster under the bed. It is not a good option.

I bring a suitcase of clothes to Ben's and a scale. Not for me, but for my food. I'm not allowed to weigh myself but I can weigh a chicken breast.

As the days pass, I try to play by the rules. I write down everything I eat in my journal. I make a note of how I feel before I eat and afterward. The process is tedious, but it is meant to keep me mindful. Checked in.

So far today I've had two slices of whole wheat toast sprayed with butter, a fine, calorie-free mist of it. Before I ate, I felt bored and hungry. After I ate, I felt bored and hungry and fat.

Ben tries to be attentive, not overbearing.

Tonight, he asks me what I want for dinner.

"Sushi?" I say. Because sushi is a safe food, not the sort of thing you'd want to binge on, stuffing wet slices of sashimi into your mouth. That doesn't sound appetizing, even to me.

We order in from a place called Crazy Fish. Here, you can get your rolls without the rice. This is how I eat almost every-thing—without the something. Burgers without the bun, salads without the dressing, sandwiches without the bread.

I've opened a bottle of wine, Two-Buck Chuck from Trader

Joe's. As I pour my second glass, Ben says, "It's wine, not water."

"It's got nice legs," I say, twirling my glass around for Ben to see.

"You've got nice legs," he says, grabbing my thigh. I pull away.

I have started to drink more than I did before, which they warned us about at the clinic. They told us we were prone to addiction, that we might trade one for the other. This is a risk I'm willing to take. If someday I become a potted housewife instead of a bulimic one, so be it.

Arriving in Italy, I'm hopeful our days will be filled with activity, distractions that will take my mind off of food. On the plane, I read the guidebooks. We have gotten all of them. Lonely Planet and Fodor's and Frommer's. The one called A Food Lover's Guide to Italy I don't bother to open.

On our first full day, we are in Piedmont following a man and his dog through the woods under the cover of night. The sun has just set and besides the moon, the burning tip of the cigarette dangling from the man's thin lips is the only light we have. His name is Ilario and he is a *trifulao*, a truffle hunter, like his father was, and his grandfather before that.

His dog, Silvana, stays close to the ground, sniffing around trees, digging intermittently. She has a scruffy black coat, the better for going undetected, Ilario tells us. If the other truffle hunters spot us, they will poach our finds—the truffles still too young to be sold—and put them back in the ground until they've matured. Truffle hunting, for all its charm and quaintness, appears to be a cutthroat business.

"*Vai, vai*," Ilario says to Silvana. Go, go.

We chase after the dog, who stops alongside a tree. The damp roots spread out like tentacles, fat and slithering, clutching at the ground. Ben bends over to catch his breath.

"You okay?" I ask. It is reassuring that occasionally Ben is not okay, that sometimes I get to be the one who is okay.

Nodding, Ben drags on his inhaler, while Silvana sniffs and circles, sniffs and circles, her tail wagging. She steps back, pleased with herself, her velvet tongue hanging out.

Meanwhile, Ilario is all business. He takes a tool from his back pocket, a small shovel, and unearths a dark, wrinkled mass, fleshy like a tumor.

Ben smells the truffle first, and then holds it under my nose. I breathe in deeply and it smells like the earth, like a man's hands after he has been working in the yard. A faint lingering odor of garlic follows. The smell isn't bad, but it's not something I would pay a thousand dollars a pound for. That's what the going rate is. For a fungus. It is impossible for me to think of food in any value other than calories.

As we walk back to the car, Ben negotiates with Ilario on the price of a single truffle from his stash. They settle on four hundred dollars for a mushroom no bigger than a tennis ball. Ben cups it gently in his palm.

"For a special occasion," he tells me.

We are staying with an old woman, breasty and wobbling, who runs something like a bed-and-breakfast in her home. We sleep in her spare bedroom and all share a single bathroom. She became indignant this morning when I didn't finish her breakfast, soft-boiled eggs and thick, iridescent slices of ham. She picked up my plate and muttered things I didn't understand.

When we return from the hunt, she admires Ben's truffle. *Magnifico*, she says to him. She doesn't even deign to glance in my direction, just makes a clicking sound when I forget to take off my boots at the door.

"She hates me," I say to Ben as we get ready for dinner, our first real meal since we arrived yesterday morning.

"You're paranoid," he tells me. He lies back on the bed and waits for me to finish dressing. I turn away from him as I take my sweater off and pull on one of my dressy tops.

Tonight will be our "nice" dinner.

It is only a short walk from the apartment to the restaurant. The place is small, with uneven plank floors and candles melting right onto the tables. Ben orders for us, pointing to the menu when the waiter can't understand his flawed Italian.

We start with the cantaloupe wrapped in prosciutto, drizzled with balsamic vinegar. Ben wants to know if I can taste its woodiness. He tells me the vinegar had been aged for more than twelve years in a chestnut barrel. And the olive oil, he says, is redolent of pears and apples.

Next we have the burrata, which Ben refers to as mozzarella's cousin. I put a glob of the wet cheese in my mouth.

"It's good," I say gamely.

"Good?" Ben says. He shakes his head. For him, good doesn't suffice, doesn't even begin to come close.

The waiter has set down our entrées and then returns holding a truffle in one hand, a grater in the other.

"No thank you," I say, holding up my hand.

Ben looks at me. "C'mon," he says.

"I'm full."

"The truffle is for taste. Tell her," he says to the waiter, hoping for an ally. "We came to Piedmont for the truffles."

The waiter says as much in his heavily accented English.

"*Un po*," I say.

The waiter deftly swipes the mushroom back and forth across the grater, as delicate shavings drift onto my pasta.

"*Bon appetit*," Ben says, his fork poised above his own meal, a steaming mound of risotto.

"Good appetite," I say. It doesn't translate. I take a deep breath and wind a noodle around my fork. The odor I had detected back on the hunt is back, cleaner now, earthy but not dirty. The pasta is slippery and smooth against my tongue and I take my time chewing it. After a few bites, I set down my fork.

Ben reaches his fork toward me. There is a pile of risotto precariously balanced on it. "Here," he says. "Try."

"No thanks." I can feel myself at the precipice. If I continue eating, I'm afraid I won't be able to stop.

"C'mon." Some of the risotto falls off his fork, landing on the table.

I lean in reluctantly, my mouth open. This will be my last bite.

"More?" he asks.

I haven't even had a chance to swallow yet. I shake my head, my lips pressed tightly together, and Ben returns to his risotto, closing his eyes as he savors each bite. When he's not looking, I raise my napkin to my mouth and discreetly spit out the food. Slowly, I work through my pasta, chewing and spitting, finishing nearly all of it. Eventually, Ben admires my plate. He smiles approvingly.

"I told you you'd love it," he says.

I nod because I want him to have this moment. He looks like a little boy whose race car has just won the Pinewood Derby.

"Dessert?" he asks, emboldened.

"Next time."

"Fair enough," Ben says. But nothing about this situation seems fair, not to me, and not to Ben either. He is being duped. The napkin, still warm and heavy as a lump of clay, sits in my lap.

The thing about hunger is that it doesn't go away. That's why a starving person will eat his dead friends to survive. It's why so many anorexics become bulimics. It's why, while Ben is sleeping, I quietly get out of bed, treading lightly on the creaky wood floors. I squat beside our suitcase, where I find a bag of pretzels left over from the flight. I suck on each one until they're soft enough to eat without making a sound. I run my wet fingertip along the inside of the bag, picking up any last crumbs and salt, the fine pieces huddled in the corners. I can feel my stomach starting to work, releasing its acids, preparing for more. It knows the drill.

I grope on the nearby nightstand, feeling for the wrinkled truffle. I bite into it as if it were a small peach. Its texture is tough, almost meaty. It only takes me a few minutes to finish it—all four hundred dollars' worth of mushroom. I don't feel full. Not stuffed. There is always room for more. But for this moment, I am satisfied.

less miserable

Your father is in the backyard brushing the horse," my mother called to tell me, as if it were the most normal thing ever. Like your father's washing the car. Or your father's mowing the lawn.

"The horse?" I asked, still in bed. Jill had already left for her run, and the phone's shrill ring, not so different from my mother's voice, had startled me awake.

"That's right," my mother said. I could tell she was waiting for me to be appalled so we could become allies, the two of us prattling on about how inane it was for there to be a horse in the backyard.

"Okay," I said, trying hard to sound unfazed. My father was dying. Prostate cancer. You make certain allowances for a sixty-six-year-old man with a full head of hair and little to no control over his equipment. That's how my father had decided to refer to it, a problem with his "equipment." For her part, my mother referred to it as "down there." "Things are not so good down there," she would say. As for me, I hardly referred to it at all.

My father kept a running journal, a gift from *Runner's World* with his purchase of a lifetime subscription. In his journal, he would draw red dots on each day there was blood in his urine.

The entries read like this: "Ran one mile. Couldn't hold down dinner." And three red dots followed, like an ellipsis.

When he started swallowing tiny plastic capsules packed with shark cartilage (because, as the book claimed, *Sharks Don't Get Cancer*), I asked my wife, Jill, what we should do. Nothing, she said. We should do nothing. The oncologist called it palliative treatment. I looked up the word in a medical dictionary. This is what it means: Death will come, only later.

"The horse bays all night," my mother continued.

"Neighs."

"What?" she asked.

"Neighs," I said. "A horse neighs."

"Isn't that what I said?"

"You said bay."

"And there's a difference?"

"Dogs bay. A horse neighs."

"Well, you're missing the point, really."

"What is the point?"

"The point is the neighbors called 911. Can you believe it? As if it were some sort of an emergency. As if it were life or death."

For all of us, everything, every choice, had become one of life or death. Even buying toilet paper was a matter of life or death. Buy it in bulk: life; one roll at a time: death.

Jill walked into the bedroom, back from her run. Wet strands of hair clung to her flushed face.

"You should hear about my father's new equine friend," I said, and Jill just shrugged, taking the phone from me.

"Hi, Mom," she said. Jill called my parents Mom and Dad. She remembered their birthdays and their anniversary. She was a better daughter-in-law than I was a son.

"Good lord," she said. "Where are you keeping it?"

I looked expectantly at her for the answer.

"In the backyard," she mouthed. "Sure," she said. "Okay. Noon is great."

———————

Jill offered to drive the twenty or so miles from our condo in Santa Monica to my parents' house in the canyons. She liked to drive. It was a control thing. We took the Pacific Coast Highway as far as we could and then wound our way through the mountains. When we reached Topanga, I rolled up the windows and flicked on the air conditioner. The car rattled, and a stale breeze sputtered from its vents, lingering for a minute before the heat overtook it.

"I hate this car," I said.

"She's seen better days," Jill said, gently patting the dashboard. I fiddled with the knob, turning the air to low, then high, as if I could trick it into working.

"Enough," Jill said. "Just leave it."

Last month the mechanic told us the car needed a new blower motor and engine bearings. Jill and I made up excuses for why we shouldn't bother repairing it. We said we needed a second opinion. We joked that the car had made it this long.

What neither of us actually said was that my father had a silver Saab 900 with little more than twelve thousand miles on it, a car he kept trying to convince us to take because my mother mostly drove them everywhere in her Honda Fit. But even thinking about that car, the possibility that it might one day be ours, felt like a betrayal, like imagining my father gone was giving the universe permission to take him.

We pulled into my parents' driveway and parked under the slender shadow of a basketball hoop, hoping for any bit of shade from the unremitting valley sun. Jill grabbed my hand and squeezed it in a way that made me self-conscious, as though she could sense I needed the support. We shuffled up to the house together, united, a team.

My father opened the door before we had a chance to knock. Jill hugged him first and I winced, worried that she might be squeezing too hard, unsettling the cancer in his body. She held on to him emphatically, for longer than you should when you're just hugging someone hello, but my father didn't seem to mind. His eyes were closed.

Then it was my turn. It had only been a couple of weeks since I had seen him last, but he already looked smaller, whiter, more rubbery. We reenacted one of those fraternity boy embraces, the kind where your chests never actually touch and there's an exaggerated show made of patting each other on the back with one hand while you shake with the other.

My mother appeared in the doorway behind my father, wearing pleated shorts that flared like bells around her legs.

"So, who wants coffee?" she asked, adding with a hint of pride that she had hazelnut creamer.

"Sold," Jill said.

We went inside, where there was fruit salad and a pyramid of bagels arranged on the kitchen table, along with all the accompaniments: sliced tomatoes and onions, whipped cream cheese, and a plate of glistening smoked salmon.

I peered through the kitchen window into the backyard, and sure enough, there was the horse. He seemed smaller than I would have expected, more like a pony.

"Sit," my mother said. "Eat."

The food had been arranged on the lazy Susan, a quaint accessory courtesy of my mother, who was fond of quaint accessories. We ceremoniously spun it around, pausing intermittently and preparing our plates.

Jill scooped out her bagel, leaving a pile of bread on the edge of her plate. She called herself a careful eater. As if eating could be hazardous.

"Did you tell your son about UCLA?" my mother asked my father, who sat there, spreading cream cheese on his bagel. I knew he would be lucky if he was able to eat it. He'd been having trouble keeping his food down. It was ironic, really, to have a father who was trying to keep food in and a wife who was trying to keep food out.

My father ignored my mother's question.

"Your father's going to UCLA," she said. "When he dies. They'll pick him up in a van and take him away, just like that."

"Huh," I said.

My father set down his bagel and cleared his throat. "I'm leaving my body to science," he said slowly, giving us time to let the idea sink in. "I don't want a burial or any of that business. Your mother's disappointed. She had already started rehearsing the eulogy."

"I did not," my mother said. "Tell your son that's not true." My parents did this. They spoke of me in the third person as if I weren't even there.

"He knows I'm teasing," my father said. "The grieving is for the living, so you guys do whatever you want. Have a party. I'm finally getting into med school." He laughed a little at his own joke.

"Well, I think it's admirable," Jill said, and my father thanked her for her support.

"Whatever makes you happy," my mother said. She reached for my father's face and wiped away a smudge of cream cheese on his chin.

I bit into my bagel and chewed while Jill looked at me expectantly, waiting for my response.

"What?" I said, barely intelligible through my mouthful.

Jill shook her head. I had let her down. Of course, she would say that I was really letting myself down. Jill was a therapist. She had a sign in her office that said, "Success comes in CANS, not CAN'TS."

"If you'll excuse me," said my father, neatly folding his napkin, leaving it behind on his way to the bathroom.

I had come to expect this, my father excusing himself from the table and the rest of us carrying on as if everything were perfectly fine. A man could use the bathroom without it being a big deal, without all of us wringing our hands in worry.

I forked a spongy piece of cantaloupe and did my best to think about tomorrow, when Jill and I would wake up next to each other and take turns showering, when we'd maybe even shower together, although probably not—we were past that stage. If nothing else, it would be just the two of us, living out our little life twenty miles from here, in a place where everything could be made to feel okay.

"I can make mimosas," my mother said, apropos of nothing.

"Okay," Jill said.

I put my arm around her tiny waist. She had on a souvenir *Les Misérables* T-shirt and I fiddled with the fabric, which felt like silk between my fingers, like second skin. When I was a kid, I thought the musical was "Less Miserable." Less miserable than what, I always wondered.

My mother got out two crystal flutes and filled them with white wine and OJ.

"We don't have champagne," she apologized.

"No biggie," Jill said, taking her flute and clinking it against my mother's.

"*Salute.*"

"*Salute,*" said my mother, affecting an accent the way she did at restaurants when she ordered her food in a bastardized Italian, the vestiges of a summer spent in Italy some thirty years ago.

"Someone should check on Dad," I said, throwing my napkin onto the plate.

"Would you?" my mother asked, turning toward me and refilling her glass with only wine.

Jill put her hand on my shoulder. "Go," she said. "Your mom and I can entertain ourselves."

I am the man, I thought. I am the son. So I went, terrified that

I would find my father, pale and sweaty, crumpled over the toilet bowl and clutching his gut.

"You all right in there, big guy?" I asked, knocking on the door. No answer. "Dad?" I said, sounding more desperate than I had intended. I braced myself and pushed the door open only to find that the bathroom was empty. It smelled like apples and cinnamon, a scent aerosolized from a can.

I walked out of the bathroom and found my father in the backyard sitting on his horse. It wasn't a pony, I realized. The horse was standing in a ditch, perfectly content, not even trying to hoof his way out.

"This here is Whistling Dixie, Del Mar Stakes Champion 1996," my father said. He was smiling, patting the horse's neck. The horse blinked at me but didn't move.

"Don't you need a permit for this?" I asked.

"Just a fence and at least an acre of land."

"Where did you get him? He is a him, right?"

"A Thoroughbred, in fact. Your mother and I bid on him at an auction out in Hemet. They were going to grind him up and send him to Europe or Asia. He'd be a hamburger. A hundred hamburgers. It's unconscionable."

I put my hand on Whistling Dixie. His coat was black and hot to the touch. A flop of mane fell down over his eyes, giving him a feminine, almost coquettish look. I stared, trying to understand him the way people are supposed to understand horses, or maybe it's the other way around.

"You keep him in a ditch?" I asked.

"This is it for him," my father said.

"He's dying?"

"I could say we're all dying, but I won't."

"You already did."

"Smart aleck," my father said.

"Seriously," I said. It was a request. I needed to make sense of what the hell was going on here.

"Seriously, he's in his grave. You have to get a horse into it when he can still walk."

"Where do you learn this stuff?"

"The Internet."

Of course, I thought.

Maybe it was the heat or the salmon or the unfortunate combination of the two, but I felt dizzy standing there in front of my dying father, who was sitting on his dying horse, like a retired general on one last ride.

"He's going in peace," I said, squatting to the ground.

"How's that?"

"Two hooves down, killed in battle," I said. "Three hooves down, wounded in battle. All hooves down, died in peace."

That's what my father—a history buff, a reader of massive tomes about Civil War generals and battles—told me about the horse-and-rider statues in Gettysburg, where he took me when I was eight or nine, young enough that I still wanted to play hide-and-seek, to crouch behind a cannon and wait to be found. We saw all the battlefields on the East Coast that trip. I came home with a lead bullet in my pocket. You could still see the teeth marks where a man had bitten down so hard while his gangrenous limb was sawed off. I looked at my father and wondered why it wasn't possible to cut out the rotten, diseased part of him.

"Don't do that," he said. I had been picking at the grass, ripping it out of the dirt, and scattering it around me.

I apologized, but my father was looking behind me now, over my head, back at the house. I turned around and could make out Jill and my mother dancing in the living room to what sounded like "Hang On Sloopy" playing from the jukebox—the same one that we had playing at my bar mitzvah more than fifteen years ago. Through the screen door, Jill and my mother looked fuzzy, like an old black-and-white movie. My mother held Jill's hand and spun in, and out, and in again. Then they held each other and swayed.

LESS MISERABLE

"Did you know this is how a horse gets to his grave?" my father asked me.

I ran my palm back and forth over the grass, as if blessing it.

"Once a horse is near death," he said, using the didactic voice he reserved for these occasions, "a sufficiently large enough grave can be dug, and assuming the horse is well enough to walk, he settles into it. They say death comes after a few days, a week at most. He'll get up there," he said, cocking his chin to the sky, "long before me."

My father knew everything. He could tell you how to get a patent or trim a tree. He could tell you the difference between AM and FM radio, and how to make a Manhattan. He could tell you Kirk Douglas's real name and when the rain was coming. And he could tell you about God. He always said that Albert Einstein believed in God—or at least some sort of higher, not necessarily anthropomorphic power. It's not the kind of God you can pray to before the big game, he used to say. This is the everywhere-and-nowhere God. The incomprehensible, something-greater-than-ourselves God.

Because even with all the synapses and cells and neurons, there's nothing to explain what makes any of us alive or dead.

At the end of the day, what I wondered about wasn't the difference between alive and dead. That I got. That made sense. What didn't make sense was the process of dying, the slow and steady deterioration of a body, the waiting in a grave for death to come. I preferred a type of death that was swift and unexpected, death that didn't ask you to be a coconspirator in the whole process, like my father had become. I lay down on the grass. The stiff, just-trimmed blades prickled against my warm skin.

"Why doesn't he climb out?" I asked my father, squinting up at him and Whistling Dixie, who shook his regal head, lengthening his neck and then relaxing it again.

"He's tired," my father explained, wiping the sweat from his forehead. His shirt was soaked through, translucent against his

55

skin, showing his breasts, soft and fleshy like an overweight ado-
lescent girl's. This was a side effect of the treatments, the drugs
that he had taken to suppress his hormones, the male ones, the
ones that were to blame.

"Do you think he knows?" I asked my father.

"Knows what?"

"That he's dying?"

"What's there to know?"

When I got home from the office a couple weeks later, Jill greeted
me at the door. "I just got off the phone with your mother," she
said.

It sounded like the way bad news begins, with this sort
of vague proclamation, ominous in its lack. Jill reached for my
hands and held them in hers. "He's gone," she said. "Whistling
Dixie."

"Jesus," I said, pulling away. "Do you have to be so dramatic?"

"I thought you might care," she said, brushing her hair self-
consciously behind her ear.

"I have a lot to care about right now."

Jill said the funeral was tomorrow. My father had insisted on
it. Nothing major. Just Jill and me and my parents. He won't have
a funeral, but for the horse, it's the whole enchilada.

"Your mother told us to wear black," Jill added.

My parents had covered the mirrors, draped them in old floral
sheets.

"We must ignore our physicality," my mother said, nodding solemnly at the mirror in the entryway. She was dressed
in a drab black dress that hung loosely on her small frame. She
looked almost otherworldly, if that's the right word. Biblical.
Somehow wise. Her lips were parched and faded, not their

usual glossy pink, and her eyes, without makeup, were only wrinkled slits.

"You look nice," she said to Jill, who was wearing a black cotton sundress that tied around her waist.

"Physicality," I said to my mother.

"Well, she does," my mother said defensively.

"Thanks," Jill said. "If it makes you feel any better, I didn't try."

"To look so good without trying," my mother said, shaking her head ruefully. She linked her arm with Jill's and then reached for my arm, holding it at the elbow. She stood there between the two of us.

"Are we ready?" she said.

"To the old man," I said in a thunderous voice, trying for levity. My mother steered us toward the backyard, past the table of food, where there were cookies, pink and green ones shaped like seashells and dipped in chocolate; cakes dripping with white icing so sugary that it made your teeth hurt just to look at them; and wobbly red and orange Jell-O molds. My mother pointed out the sponge cake, which she said was lowfat.

"I wanted to get strawberries, but they didn't look good," she added.

When we got outside, my father was on the lawn rocking back and forth, shifting his weight from one foot to the other. It looked as if he was praying, although we weren't a family that prayed, at least not in the traditional way. My father called modern-day Judaism a racket, with its valet parking at the synagogue and High Holy Day tickets being hocked on eBay. Even rabbis now had their own reality TV shows.

"The kids are here," my mother said. Even though Jill and I were thirty-three and thirty-four respectively, we would forever be referred to as "the kids."

Jill mouthed "I'm so sorry" to my father.

I shrugged. A horse died, literally keeled over in his own grave. My father shrugged back, not for lack of anything better to say, but because he was a man who didn't like anyone to feel awkward, or uncomfortable, or left out.

"He was a good horse," my father said.

My mother nodded in agreement. This animal had been with my parents for less than a month, and now everyone was pretending it was some sort of life-changing experience. I breathed in deeply, looked up at the blindingly white sky. Jill moved closer to me.

Whistling Dixie was in his grave, a white sheet spread over him, revealing the shape of his body, legs tucked in, fetal almost. My father sat down by the side of the grave, his legs dangling into it.

"What are you doing?" my mother asked.

"It's not right to bury him like this," he said, shaking his head, frustrated. He told us the body needed to be fully covered. It was disrespectful to do anything less.

My father hopped into the grave and carefully rearranged the sheet, covering a barely exposed hoof. When he was satisfied, he pressed his palms against the ground above him, attempting to hoist himself out of the grave.

"Help your father," my mother whispered after a few moments. Jill gently nudged me and I lowered myself to the ground. At first, my father tried to shoo me away, telling me he was fine. But then he complied, his body going slack. I reached my hands under his arms and lifted him up, while my mother whispered behind me: "Careful, careful. Easy now." Once my father was standing again, he brushed the dirt off his pants and shirt, sending swirls of dust into the air.

"Okay then," he said. "I guess we start."

He formally thanked Jill and me for coming. He thanked my mother for being a good sport about the whole thing. He knew this wasn't easy for her, he said. And then he spoke about Whistling Dixie. He was only twenty-two, my father said. This detail made me jealous. It was one thing for the horse to take such possession of my father when I thought of the horse as old and wise. But to be only twenty-two and have so much credibility when I felt like I had none didn't seem right. Later, Jill would tell me that I was being childish. Sibling rivalry with a horse.

When my father was done eulogizing Whistling Dixie, he turned to the rest of us. "Would anyone else like to say a few words?" he asked.

"Me," I said softly. I didn't have anything planned, didn't know what I would say, but it seemed as if I should speak. It was a chance to prove something, to show I was capable of being capable.

"Okay," my father said, clapping his hands together, a little too pleased given the somber occasion.

I cleared my throat and began. "I didn't know Whistling Dixie that well. It would have been nice to spend more time with him. He had a good life, a full life."

These were all the clichés I had at my disposal for such occasions. I kicked at the dirt. I looked at my father, who nodded in an encouraging way, as if I were at bat, like the count was three and two, bases loaded.

"It doesn't really seem fair," I continued. "That he should die. In fact, it seems ridiculous to me. Death is ridiculous. This whole thing is ridiculous."

Nobody said anything. They all watched me, waiting to see if I was done. But I wasn't done. I picked up the shovel and began scooping dirt into the grave.

My father grabbed my wrist and told me it was okay.

I stood there waiting to feel whatever it was acceptance felt like. My mother and Jill stood with their bodies against each other, holding each other up, while my father and I took turns. We rolled up our sleeves and passed the shovel between us, saying nothing, watching as the earth covered the horse little by little, until finally the ground rose up to meet us, and Whistling Dixie was gone.

beverly hills adjacent

You should know that this has always been a nice neighborhood, a respectable place to raise a family. My wife and I, we raised our two daughters here and they turned out just fine, although one is now on a boat in some sea or gulf, and the other lives in Orange County with her husband, a fellow who does yoga and makes you take off your shoes at the door.

I don't visit much.

But that is beside the point. The point is we are not in Beverly Hills, but we are very close to it, spitting distance, if you will. It's an area known as Beverly Hills Adjacent, and on a good day, when my knee isn't giving me trouble, I can walk to the Coffee Bean and Tea Leaf on Beverly in under ten minutes, no problem.

It's a nice neighborhood, like I said. People take good care of their lawns, they pick up after their dogs, they put their Christmas lights up after Thanksgiving and take them down right after New Year's. So to see what has happened here in recent months, well, it's the kind of thing that would make a man do something crazy.

When all of this business first began, I said, well, at least it's not on my street. Then it happened a block away, and I said, well, at least I don't have to see it every day. And then, wouldn't you know it, one morning I wake up to find it happening right outside my window, just across the way.

"Would you look at that," I say to no one in particular. I've lived alone since my wife, Mena, passed. Mena from Palestina. This is what I called her, although she was from Texas, not Palestina. But that's beside the point. The point is I welcome all types of people. There is a Japanese woman and her black husband who live across the street. Isaac and Keiko Mullins. And the house on the corner, that one is occupied by two nice young men and their little dog. I've seen rats bigger than that animal of theirs, but who am I to judge? It's not my business.

But here is where I draw the line and say enough is enough. We've got people moving into my neighborhood and demolishing perfectly nice homes so they can build their marble and stucco monstrosities with their columns and their balconies and their big arched doorways. There is a name for these sorts of homes. It's not meant to be a nice name, I will warn you. They are called Persian Palaces. I, for one, have nothing against the Persians as a people. Their taste in architecture, that's another thing altogether.

If Mena were here, she'd say I'm overreacting. So I decide maybe she's right. Maybe it's a simple remodel. Maybe they'll run out of money. Maybe there'll be an earthquake. I'm a patient man. So I let the weeks go by. That, I tell you, was my first mistake. Because eventually, it's worse than I ever suspected. When the home starts to look like a Vegas casino, I run clear out of patience.

I go to Kinko's—it's a twenty-four-hour establishment—and I make some flyers. "ATTENTION," I write across the top. "Stop the mansionization of our neighborhood. New homes pose a serious threat." Exclamation point. Exclamation point. "Urgent meeting," I wrote, and gave them all the pertinent details.

Next, I ride my bicycle around the neighborhood and place these flyers in mailboxes and on windshields. I feel it is my civic duty to spread the word. Before the meeting, I go to Trader Joe's because I'm not too proud to seek out a good bargain. At home, I set out some mixed nuts and blintzes with not real cheese but the tofu kind, which they say is good for you, and I'm just foolish enough to believe them. I brew a pot of coffee, decaf given the hour. There's a bottle of wine in the refrigerator if anyone cares for something a little stiffer, although I don't think this is a neighborhood of heavy drinkers.

The meeting is called for 6:30 p.m. and, at nearly eight, I'm still sitting there alone, watching *Jeopardy!* As luck would have it, I fall asleep on the couch and when I wake up it's after ten o'clock. Well, I'm no dummy. I know when to call it quits. Perhaps there was a big game on tonight. I don't follow sports, but for all I know, the Lakers are in the World Series or whatever nonsense it is. I hear that Kobe Bryant is something else, a fine athlete.

The next day, as usual, construction across the street starts bright and early at seven o'clock. Now, I'm not a late sleeper, but that's beside the point. The point is I could be. And then what?

The workers start in with the banging and the drilling and the hooting and hollering, a bunch of illegals as far as I can tell. Cheap labor. I'm practically doing them a favor, walking over there and shutting down this operation.

"Who's the turkey in charge here," I demand. I'm still wearing my bathrobe and slippers to help make my case. One of the men saunters on up to me. He's got a tool belt around his waist and I suppose he thinks that makes him a bona fide professional.

"Is there a problem?" he asks.

A problem? He wants to know if there's a problem. Well, I go ahead and count to ten like my doctor told me to do. According to him, it's better for the ticker this way. So, fair enough. I get to ten, and then I say what I was planning to say all along, which is this: "The problem is that you owe me one hour of sleep for every morning of clanking and banging, and a lifetime of making up for all this ugliness you're planning on having me look at."

"I get my boss," this fellow says. And I think that's a fine idea. The man who must be the boss shows up a few moments later. He's wearing a suit, an expensive-looking one at that, so I know he's not getting his hands dirty.

"You in charge here?" I ask, pointing my finger at him.

"It's my house," he says. And I can't believe my good fortune. I'm ready to let him have it.

"You, my friend, are erecting an eyesore."

He gives me the once-over, looking at my bathrobe as if this discredits my authority on the matter, which, I will tell you, it does not. I retie the robe, pulling it nice and tight under my waist. I think the gesture should speak for itself.

"My name is Feroz," he tells me. "Feroz Azzizi." He holds out his hand for me to shake, and at the end of the day, I'm still a gentleman, so I give a firm shake.

"Max," I say, introducing myself. "Max Kapler."

"A pleasure to meet you, Mr. Kapler."

"Right," I say. "A real pleasure." I'm willing to be polite, if that's what it takes. After all, my goal is not to make enemies.

"About this eyesore," I say.

"What do you mean, eyesore?"

"This house you're building. Would you believe that it literally hurts my eyes?"

"No," he says. "I really and truly cannot believe it."

Well, I see how it's going to be. I start counting to ten.

"Max," Feroz says to me once I get to eight. "May I call you Max?"

"Why not?"

"Max, let's go inside. I have not yet had my tea. We will drink first and then we will talk."

Oh, we'll talk all right, I say to myself. I can assure you that I'm only getting started.

We walk inside the house, right through the big arched opening since there's no door yet. I can't believe my eyes. Everywhere marble and gold, on the floors and the staircase and the ceiling. I follow Feroz into the kitchen, where he's already got a pot of tea set up on some makeshift contraption. He pours two glasses and hands one to me.

"It's quite hot," he says. I bet it is. I grab the glass and take a sip to let him know that a little heat doesn't scare me.

"Please," he says, motioning toward a box on the floor. "Sit." He tells me that his sink is inside this box. Marble, he says, which doesn't impress me one bit. I hop on and the shame of it is my feet barely touch the ground. But what can I do? I'm not a tall man.

Feroz takes a seat on the box across from me. "The dishwasher," he says, rubbing his hand along the cardboard. He's smiling at me so I smile back.

"I am building this house for my wife," he says. He takes his wallet out and shows me a photograph.

"Not bad," I say. It's true. She reminds me of a movie star. Not Rita Hayworth. Not Greta Garbo. Ach. I can't think of the name. My wife would know. She loved the pictures.

"You are married?" Feroz says to me. He stands up so he can return his wallet to his back pocket.

I get on my feet too, just to keep things even.

"For fifty-two years," I say, and Feroz nods, impressed.

This was no small feat. I loved my wife, but we had our disagreements from time to time. She told me I drove too fast and ate too slow. She thought I was a lousy dancer and a bad dresser. So fine, I stopped dancing and I let her pick out my clothes. A marriage is about compromise.

But why are we talking about this? This man is clever, trying to distract me. I'm not so easily had.

"Feroz," I say. "I think you should know that this house does not belong here."

"Where does it belong?"

"My friend," I say, because I want him to know I've got his

best interest in mind. "Where it belongs is anywhere else, as far as I'm concerned."

Feroz nods like he's thinking this over. "Max," he says, "I'm fairly certain it's not possible to move my house. And even if I could, I can assure you my wife would not allow it. She is fond of this neighborhood."

"Ava Gardner," I say. The name just came to me.

"I am sorry?"

"Nothing," I say. I need a moment to collect my thoughts. The older I get, the more my mind wanders, goes off in its own direction. One minute I'm thinking about what to have for dinner and the next I'm remembering the time I got thrown in jail in Tijuana. I set my glass of tea down on the counter and hop off the box. I think better on my feet than on my fastaffus.

"Feroz, tell me. Where are you from?"

"Cleveland," he says.

"And before that?"

"I was born in Iran."

"Now, how would you like it if I came to Iran and knocked down one of your fine houses and built my own place. I'm talking a real American home, with shutters on the windows and a white picket fence. The works. What would you think about that?" I'm feeling good now. I'm on a roll.

"I'm not sure I understand."

So I repeat the whole thing again for him, this time more slowly, because I want to make sure he's able to grasp the point that I'm making. And he tells me that he still does not get it.

I point my finger at him and tell him to think about it. Think long and hard, I say. As I walk out the doorway that has no door, Feroz calls after me.

"Max," he says. "I am sorry to see a neighbor so upset. I hope one day you will come over for dinner. My wife's beauty is matched only by her talents in the kitchen."

"Ach," I say, wishing I had a door to slam.

What I am about to tell you is not something I am proud of. I had tried to reason with Feroz, but he would not have it. So now what I want is a small bit of revenge. I take what I can get.

I sit in my house and I wait for the day to end. I make a pot of coffee, stronger than rocket fuel and blacker than black. Two cups later, the construction workers have finally gone back to wherever it is they came from. But I continue to wait. I wait until my neighbors have turned the lights off in their houses. I use the facilities and then I wait some more. For a man in my situation, this wait is never a long while. When the feeling comes, I run as fast as I can, which is not so fast given the lousiness of my knee. I hurry across the street and, for a moment, I'm afraid I won't make it. When I get to the door that has no door, there is now a door. But this cannot stop me. I must go through with the plan and I'm running out of time, so I sneak around and find a window with no window. I suddenly feel light on my feet, and I'm able to hoist myself up and through the opening, no problem. Once I am inside, I look for my spot. I know I'm running out of time. My bladder is growing impatient, so fine. I decide to do my business right there in whatever room I'm in. I pull my equipment out and empty my tank.

That night, I sleep like a baby, best sleep I've had in years even with all the coffee I drank, if you can believe it. I don't wake up until after ten, and the first thing I do is check in on the eyesore. I cannot believe what I see. I go to the door and open it so I can step outside to get a better view. Feroz notices me and waves.

"Picket fence," he yells, pointing to the posts that are being shoved into the dirt. It's a picket fence all right. White slats wrapping around the front yard of his marble palace.

So I think that this business of the white picket fence is Feroz trying to stick it to me, and he's sure done a good job of it. Still, the way I see it, he may have won the battle, but this war is not yet over. I need to think about my next move. I don't want to do anything rash. This is going to require a strategy. I'm a military man. Mena liked to remind me that I worked in the mess hall in Guam, but it's still something. I know how to conduct myself in desperate situations.

Before I do anything I eat my oatmeal, which is how I like to start the morning. A big bowl of oatmeal with brown sugar and raisins. It's the kind of breakfast that makes you feel like the world isn't such a bad place to be. Mena used to make it for me from scratch, but now that she's gone, I get the instant variety pack from the grocery store and prepare it myself in the micro-wave. Two packs I use.

After the oatmeal, I consider my options. I can march myself across the street and try, once again, to reason with Feroz. Of course, I'm no glutton for punishment. I see how well reasoning worked the first time, so I decide to try another tactic. I'm going to the media. This is what I should have done in the first place. If you want to get noticed in this day and age, you've got to be on TV.

Here is the letter I type up to send to the local news stations. On the envelope, I write "Breaking News," so they know to take the matter seriously.

Dear Kind Sir or Madam:

I know that in your line of business you're always looking for a scoop, and have I got one for you. Perhaps you are aware of recent events in the Beverly Hills Adjacent area, zip code 90212. What we have here is an age-old story of tradition versus change. Now, I'm all for change of the positive nature. I've used the computer at my public library, where I'm a regular, mind you. I'm a big supporter of the public facilities. But the kind of change I'm referring to here is for the worse. I'm not one to exaggerate, but I would say that what is happening is a tragedy. A real tragedy.

So let me get to the point, as I'm sure your time is precious. News waits for no one, right? That's why I advise you to come see for yourself. See what has happened. The destruction of homes. While I can't say for certain that these homes are historic landmarks, I will tell you they've been here as long as I have and that's no small thing.

These homes, perfectly nice places to live, are being reduced to piles of rubble and carted off in Dumpsters. In their place, you will find marble columns and golden statues, houses the size of hotels. How can this be stopped? How can we save our neighborhoods? I will be honest. I do not have the answer. But one thing I know for sure is that we must act fast. We must come together and fight the good fight.

I maintain a flexible schedule and am available for interviews at your convenience. From sunup to sundown, I will be in front of the house located across the street from me at 427 Wooster Street. You won't be able to miss it.

Sincerely yours,
Max P. Kapler
Local Resident

The *P* in Max P. Kapler is just for effect. I don't have a middle name, but I think it sounds more important this way. I go to the post office myself because I don't have a good feeling about the mailman. He's always saying good morning and waving and if I had to guess, I'd say he's on something, perhaps he has gotten himself into the drugs. So no problem. I can get to the post office on my own.

Once I've mailed my letters, I go home and call my daughter, the one in Orange County. Perhaps I failed to mention that she's a sex therapist, if you can believe it. She tells me she's providing a service and I don't even want to think about what kind of service it is. In my day, you got it on the corner, not in a doctor's office. But fine. She has a master's degree, so I guess that counts for something.

I call her up on her mobile phone, because she says this is the best way to reach her. In fact, she got me one of those gadgets for my eighty-second birthday, so now I've got a mobile phone even though I'm not all that mobile. I don't even know how to turn the thing on.

She doesn't answer, but a voice that's not my daughter's, that much I know, tells me to press one if I want to leave a message or wait for the beep. I wait for the beep.

I leave a message that goes something like this: "Ruthie. Hello. Is this thing working? It's your father. I'm calling to let you know that things here are not good. We have a situation. It's under control. But I do want you to know that we definitely have a situation. So if anything happens to me, and I'm not saying anything will, but if anything does, you remember this name: Feroz. You got that? Feroz. Okay. I'm hanging up now."

I leave the message as a precaution. I don't know what kind of trouble I might get into. Better safe than sorry, as Mena liked to say. She was always very practical. Very levelheaded. She clipped coupons and sent birthday cards. That's the kind of woman she was.

Mena picked out the suit I intend to put on as part of my plan. I haven't worn the suit since her funeral. It's the only one I've got. From Sears. It was $120 and that was on sale. But Mena said it was a good investment, a nice polyester blend that would never go out of style.

I figure if I wear the suit, Feroz will have to take me more seriously. He'll see that I'm no longer playing games. The next morning, I wake up before the construction workers arrive. It's still dark outside, just before six. I put my suit on along with my dress shoes, also selected by Mena. My swollen feet fit into them only on a good day, and, thank God, today is a good day. I have my oatmeal and I get a folding chair out of the garage.

And here's what I do: I plant myself right in front of the picket fence. I'm not going to budge. If anyone wants in, he will have to go through me, Max Kapler. As the workmen start arriving in their beat-up trucks, I give them the eye. I don't get up. I'm taking this one step at a time.

There's about five of them now. They're standing in a huddle by the driveway with their arms folded across their chests. I hear them speaking their fast Spanish.

"That's right," I yell at them. "Nobody goes in."

So one of them has the nerve to come up to me. "Halt," I say, putting my hand out. "I cannot permit you to enter."

"Mister," he says to me. "We have work to do."

"Not today," I say. "Not on my watch. No sir."

He sort of shrugs and backs away. Just as I thought. These fellows are happy to take the day off. So they pile in their trucks and drive away. But I don't budge. I know they might be going to get reinforcements. And as I suspected, about two hours later, once the sun is right above me, beating down on my head, they drive by again, slowing down in front of the house. I wave them on. "Keep going," I say. "There's no work for you here."

I don't know how much time passes. I fall asleep, my head flopping forward. There's a nice enough breeze so I don't get too hot. When I'm awake, I watch the people pass by in their cars, most of them not even noticing me, an old man in a suit sitting in front of a picket fence. The neighbors with the rat-dog walk by together, the two men holding hands. I look away because that's not something I need to see.

"Everything okay, Mr. Kapler?" one of them says. The little rat-dog is growling at me. The other fellow talks to the animal like it's a person, saying, "Hush, Bunny. It's just Mr. Kapler." A dog that looks like a rat with a name like Bunny. It's too much.

But now that I have the attention of these two men, I decide

I'll let them in on my plan. Perhaps they could be allies. Stranger things have happened. I tell them I've alerted the media, that it's only a matter of time before they show up. I'm going to put a stop to this mansionization one way or another. I want to add, if it's the last thing I do. But that seems a little dangerous, like tempting death. No thank you.

"So?" I say to them. "Are you in or are you out?"

They look at each other, as if they're trying to decide which one of them should do the talking. "Well, Max," the taller one says. "We sympathize with your position. But I think we, you know, we'd prefer not to get involved."

He looks at his friend, who nods in agreement.

"Just wait until it's across the street from your house," I say. "You could be next. You'll see."

They tell me to have a nice day and continue walking with their little rat-dog prancing out in front. So fine. I can take care of this business on my own.

When I see Feroz arrive in his fancy silver Mercedes, I straighten my tie and smooth a hand over the little hair I've got left.

"Good afternoon, Max," he says to me.

"Afternoon," I say, staying right where I am, in front of the gate, not budging. I plan to hold my ground. No matter what. The only way I'm leaving is in handcuffs, and like I said, a jail cell doesn't scare me. Not after that night in Tijuana when they threw me in the slammer for being drunk and disorderly. I danced pantless in a fountain. So sue me. I was young and in love. Mena bailed me out. If she were here now, she'd probably be making a scene herself, telling me to get myself back inside and stop acting like a crazy old man.

When Feroz asks me what I'm doing in front of his house, I tell him that I'm here in protest.

"Protest against what?"

"I think you know."

"Please, Max. How can we remedy this situation?"

"You can put the house back that was once here. It was light blue, one story, shingles on the roof."

"I think you know that's not going to happen."

"I know no such thing."

"Try to be reasonable," he says to me, and I start counting to ten because it's the only thing I can do to keep from losing it. He keeps on talking, going on about how the house is nearly done. And the picket fence, he's using that against me now. "For you," he says to me, "we put the picket fence in. We, my wife and I, thought this was a nice compromise."

I feel a little dizzy on account of the fact that I have low blood sugar and haven't had a moment to eat since the oatmeal, but I can't let that distract me. "A nice compromise," I say. "My foot."

"Perhaps tomorrow after a good night's rest, we can talk again. It is too late to begin working today anyway."

"That's a fine plan," I say. Although I don't trust this man. He might be trying to pull a fast one, so once he's gone I sit back down in my chair and decide I'm not moving. The only time I get up is to use the facilities. Like I said before, I don't feel great about urinating in that house, no matter how ugly it is, and try as I might, I can't bring myself to do it again. I jog to my house and jog back. I stay in the chair all night. Sure, it cools off once the sun goes down, but I'm a man with a mission. The elements are no match against my will.

The next day, the Mexican workers show up right on time. They see me sitting there and I shoo them on once again. "Don't bother," I say. But they park their trucks and get out, carrying their tools with them.

"Hey there," I say. I'm on my feet now. "You guys go ahead and take the day off. We're closed for business."

The same guy, sort of heavy with a mustache, comes up to me. "We don't work, we don't get paid."

I'm a sympathetic man. I know what it's like to be out of

work, to be struggling to feed a family, so I see if maybe I can make a deal with these guys. They tell me they get paid twelve dollars an hour and there are six of them working eight-hour days.

"Give me a second," I say, and I try to calculate the numbers in my head. As I'm doing the math, my mind starts to do its wandering thing again, and now I'm thinking about how I was never a very good student. I met Mena in high school. She sat next to me in geometry and let me cheat off her, and boy was she smart. She'd be able to do this math in her head, no problem. As for me, I'm writing on my pants with my finger, trying to picture the numbers so I can figure this business out. If I've done it right, each worker makes about a hundred dollars per day, and I've got $5,786 in my sock drawer. So I tell the Mexican in charge that I will pay them for the day's work if they drive off, spend the day with their families or at a bar, I don't care, as long as they're not here. "Have we got a deal?" I ask.

"If we leave, that's it. We're fired." He runs his finger across his throat like he's slitting it.

"Okay," I say, "nobody's getting fired." I tell him I'm a close personal friend of Feroz and I'll make sure everything is taken care of. A man in my position has to think on his feet. I have the Mexican, we'll call him José, I have José sit in my chair, while I dart across the street to get the six hundred dollars.

I count it out, paying each of them for a day's work. José shakes my hand and tells me thank you. *Muchas gracias,* he says.

I must have fallen asleep for a while, because the next thing I know, I'm awake, and beside my chair there's a bottle of water and a plate covered in tinfoil. I kick the plate a little with my foot, just to be safe. It could be a bomb, for all I know. When nothing happens, I bend over and pull back the tinfoil, only the edge of it, to see what I'm getting myself into. Rice. I'm getting myself into rice. Perhaps this is a bribe on the part of Feroz. But so what if it is? I figure I can still eat the rice and hold my ground. After all, I haven't eaten since my oatmeal yesterday.

The giver of the rice has thought to leave a fork behind as well. If I wasn't so angry, I'd be grateful. The rice is good, I will admit. In addition to the rice, which I finish quickly, I discover a layer of potatoes, sliced and fried. I never met a potato I didn't like. Fried, baked, mashed, you name it. And these potatoes are no different. If Mena were here, I'd have her get the recipe.

I always want to sleep after a meal, so once I'm done I shut my eyes. Just for a bit, I think. I only want to recharge myself. What happens next must be by the grace of God, because when I open my eyes, I see a news van parked across the street. Channel 11, it says. I am overjoyed. Victory feels near.

A woman in a bright red suit walks over to me. "Are you Mr. Kapler?"

"Indeed, I am," I say.

"I'm Donna Crane. My producer got your letter. We're thinking this would make a good human-interest story. Something a little lighter after the hard news, the fires and whatnot."

If this isn't hard news, I don't know what is, but I can't be picky. So I say okay, let's do it. This Donna waves over a bunch of people and next thing I know someone's brushing powder on my face.

"Is that makeup?" I say.

This girl, who can't be more than twenty, tells me it's something to take the shine off.

"Oh no," I say. "I'm not going on TV wearing makeup."

"You won't be able to tell. Trust me. All the men do it."

Well, I'm not all the men, but fine. What's done is done. Another young gal comes over. She tells me she's the producer.

"Do you have any signs? I think the shot would be better if we had signs." I just put my hands up and look around to show her that, as she can see, there are no signs. So she gets on her phone and talks to someone about these signs she's so keen on.

"What do you want them to say?" she says. And I think she's still talking to the person on the other end of the phone, so I keep my mouth shut, but then she says, "Mr. Kapler, what would you like the signs to say?"

I think for a moment. "Mansionization is destroying our neighborhood."

"Okay," she says. "That's good." She repeats it back into the phone.

"Too long," she says to me. "We can't fit 'mansionization' and 'neighborhood.'"

So get a bigger sign, I think.

"All right," she says, holding the phone to her ear. " 'Mansions must go.' That's good. Gets the point across."

I like my idea better, but I figure these are professionals. They know what they're doing. Everything happens so fast. Someone comes over with the signs and I've got one on each side of me, and a third one they give me to hold. This sign says "Down with Persian Palaces." I know it's controversial, but this is the news. They need a good story and I'm going to give it to them.

Once the camera's rolling and Donna Crane asks me why I'm sitting in front of my neighbor's half-built house, I tell it like it is. I tell her about the history of this neighborhood, where I've been living for fifty-seven years. I tell her about the destruction, the disregard for tradition. And she's nodding the whole time. So I keep going. I tell her how I tried to reason with my neighbor. And he goes and puts up a picket fence. Who has ever seen such a thing?

"I think it's a first," Donna Crane says, and someone yells cut and the whole thing is over just like that. The real shame of it is that I can't abandon my post, so I don't get to see myself on the news, but I know my voice is finally being heard. Max P. Kapler can no longer be ignored.

The next morning, I must be dreaming, because I wake up and see Ava Gardner standing over me. She's got her dark hair pulled back and her eyebrows groomed to perfection.

"Good morning," she says to me. "You must not have slept very well."

"I can sleep anywhere," I tell her.

"You liked the rice?"

And now I realize that this isn't Ava Gardner at all. It's the wife.

"I'm not going anywhere," I tell her, collecting myself and sitting up straighter.

"You are going to sit here forever?"

"If that's what it takes."

"May I sit with you?" she says.

"Sure," I say. "Why not?" If she thinks she's going to use her womanly wiles to break me, she's got another thing coming.

"I'll be right back," she says.

She gets a chair out of the back of her car, and I know that I should get up to help her, but I'm still thinking this all might be a trick. She sets her chair down next to mine and lets out a long breath.

"It's a pretty street," she says.

"That's right," I say.

She fishes around in her purse for something and pulls out a silver tin that she sets in her lap. "Noon-Baadoomi," she says, placing her hand on it and smiling at me.

I have no idea what she's talking about, so I don't say a word. Sometimes that's the best strategy, to just keep your mouth shut.

"They're cookies. Usually for a wedding, but my husband, he loves them, so what can you do?" She opens the tin and holds it out, and I take one of her cookies. Only a starving fool turns down food. We sit like this for I don't know how long. An hour, maybe two.

"I'm Sheva," she says. This is the first we've spoken since the cookies.

"Max," I say.

"Nice to meet you."

I nod.

"My husband wanted to send the workers back today," she says to me. "You know they can get over the fence?"

"Is that so?"

"I told him there was no point. You are our neighbor. It will only make things worse." She looks at one of the signs and reads it out loud. "Down with Persian Palaces."

"I didn't write it," I say.

"But you believe it."

I don't say a word. Max P. Kapler is rarely without words, but put a beautiful woman in front of me, and yes, I sometimes falter. She smells like almonds and sugar. I take a deep breath and she keeps talking. "Your house could be painted," she says. "It's peeling in spots. You see, beneath the window."

"My house is just fine," I say.

"And the bushes in front. You know they are dead, or almost dead."

"Almost dead is nothing like dead," I say.

"I don't want to be mean. I only want you to know that I may not like to look at your house every day."

"Aha!" I say. "You agree with me, then. I don't want to look at your house and you don't want to look at mine."

"Perhaps," she says. "Although I am not sitting in front of your house with signs."

Sheva looks at the watch on her slender wrist. She tells me she has to go pick her daughter up from school. "She is only three," she says, "but already she can read. It's really something."

"Wait," I say, holding out the tin of cookies.

"Keep it. I have more at home."

I finish the cookies, every last one of them. I hold on to the

tin, because Sheva might come back for it. And I don't need her
thinking I'd try to make off with it. I watch the kids come out
all scrawny-limbed and loud, chasing each other around, riding
their bikes on the lawns. I throw my fist in the air and grunt, but
I don't have quite so much fight left in me. A man has to know
his limits.

It's starting to get dark, the kind of smoggy dark you get in
Los Angeles, when my daughter shows up and invites me to Orange County. She heard about my debut on the news. Her friends
had called. The newscasters, they referred to me as disgruntled.
"An elderly disgruntled resident tries to storm the castle," they
said. They made me into a fool.

"Maybe a little time away will help," my daughter says. She
wants me to stay with her and her husband, the yoga fanatic.

"Please?" she says. I look at my house. Mena and I bought it
for less than fifty thousand dollars. We had paid it off in thirty
years. Then Mena got sick and I took out a second mortgage.
Now, truth be told, it is more the bank's house than mine.

"Okay," I say to my daughter. "But I'm keeping my shoes on."

"Fine," she says. "Whatever makes you happy."

If only it were so simple.

dog people

We were expecting company and Adam had wanted to put Lucy outside, but Lucy wasn't an outside dog. She had never been an outside dog. Besides, it wasn't *company* company. It was Paul and his friend, his "good friend."

Paul and I had dated years ago—ages ago—when I lived in New York and had just adopted Lucy from the shelter on Ninety-second Street. While the other dogs barked desperately and shook their cages, like prisoners about to revolt, Lucy cowered in the corner. She was a puppy then, a five-month-old Lab mix with a gold coat and black eyes. The shelter said she was crate-trained. She wasn't.

Paul, Lucy, and I had all shared one bed back then. And after we broke up, he maintained visitation rights. The split had been entirely mutual. We were both in our early thirties and reasonable people. We had spent one good year together and neither of us felt ready, not marriage-ready, at least not about each other. We decided we were better off as friends and congratulated ourselves for being so mature about the whole thing.

Since then Lucy and I had moved to Los Angeles, where I met Adam. And now I was pregnant with Adam's child, and Paul was in town for a wedding. He would be coming over for drinks with his "good friend," who was probably his girlfriend or close enough to it, but Paul was forty-one and so used to being a bachelor that the best he could do was call a woman he was dating a "good friend."

"So I finally get to meet Lucy's father?" Adam said. He had opened a bottle of red wine and drank while I arranged miniquiches on a plate.

"He was more like an uncle," I said. "The fun uncle." I picked up Adam's wine and took a sip. I was seven months pregnant and had chosen to believe the studies that said moderate alcohol consumption in the third trimester was okay, as opposed to the studies that said it wasn't.

Adam opened the refrigerator and took out the prosciutto meant for our guests. Lucy, who had been hovering close to me, always angling for a scrap of food, hobbled over to him. She was seven now, which meant in dog years she was about forty, a year older than me. We were both beginning to feel our age. She had a limp, which the vet said could have come from a strain or a bruise. She may have been in pain, but appetite overruled. She sat at Adam's feet and looked up at him imploringly. This was my fault. I had spoiled Lucy from the beginning. She was my baby.

"I don't think so," Adam said, taunting her as he tilted his head back and dangled the sliver of pink meat over his mouth.

Lucy whined and let out a muffled bark, a warning bark, to let him know she was ready for a fight.

"Give her a piece," I said. "Please."

"Erin," he said, looking at me sideways, a reprimand. He called me the Enabler. But ultimately he conceded and tossed a slice across the kitchen. Lucy leapt to retrieve it, limp and all.

"Thank you," he said to her, as if she were ungrateful.

Adam wasn't a dog person, which hadn't been a surprise. It

was something I knew from the beginning, from the first time he met Lucy. You could tell by his body language, the way he twisted away from her when she came to say hello. "Hey, girl," he would say, giving her a perfunctory pat on the head before shooing her away. I used to believe that you could tell a lot about a man by how he treated a dog. Of course when my mother heard this, she said, "And the Nazis? They treated their dogs like kings."

Was that true? I didn't know. But I figured she was right, at least in principle. Not everyone had to be a dog person. There were certainly worse things. And Adam was smart and funny. He had a good job and was ready to have a family, which was more than you could say about a lot of men.

"What time are Paul and company coming?" Adam asked, refilling his glass.

"Eightish," I said, taking the first sip of his wine.

"Are we going to need more?" he asked.

"Paul drinks Scotch."

"Well, then."

Adam had never met Paul, but he pre-disliked him for the obvious reasons, the fact that I used to sleep with him, the fact that Paul was a banker, the fact that he earned a lot of money and drove a little car. Adam was of the school that looked down on "suits," anyone with a desk job and a big bank account. Adam was a producer, mostly of music videos and sports documentaries. He paid twelve dollars for a haircut and only ate sushi at small, ambience-less places where the menus were indecipherable. He was big on being real. On authenticity. He wore original Converse sneakers to prove it. I'm making fun of him now for these things, but none of them were terrible. None of them were deal-breakers.

"You look purdy," Adam said. He was standing behind me now, groping my breasts, taut and veiny, swollen from pregnancy, as I tried to array the mostly Italian meats and cheeses on a wooden cutting board. I wasn't much of a cook, but I was good at presentation.

"Stop," I said, shoving his hands away with my elbows.

"What? I'm horny."

"They're going to be here any minute."

"That's all I need."

"Seriously, Adam."

"I am serious." His hand was under my dress now as he ran a finger under the elastic of my threadbare underwear, stretched out and baggy even on my fat frame.

"Five minutes," I said.

"Ten?"

I held up my hand, wiggling my fingers, which had become like sausages with all the water I was retaining. "Five," I said.

He brought my hand to his lips, kissed it, and led me into the living room, where we settled our bodies onto the stiff leather couch that rustled under our weight. Sex had become well choreographed and routine now that I was seven months pregnant. Me in front, Adam in back. My skirt around my waist, his pants at his knees. My hands at my side, his on my breasts. At the foot of the couch, I could see Lucy, her head sitting on the armrest as she watched intently. When we made eye contact, she snorted, whinnying horselike. As he continued moving inside of me, Lucy began barking her hey-what-about-me bark, pausing after each yelp to gauge our reaction.

"Adam," I said.

I could feel his breath against my ear, the pace quickening.

"Adam, I can't." I was dry now. There was no point. I edged my body away from him.

He sat up and shoved Lucy away from the couch. "This is ridiculous," he said, yanking up his jeans. Once he left the room, I quietly called for Lucy to come.

"Hi, baby," I said.

Six months ago, when Adam and I moved into the house in Valley Glen, Lucy had been kicked out of the bed and onto the floor. It was a condition of our cohabitation. We both made concessions. Adam couldn't put up his Elvis Costello posters or smoke cigarettes out the window. And Lucy couldn't sleep at the foot of the bed, curled up by our feet. Fine. Fair enough. I got her a soft fleece doggy bed that stayed on the floor in our room. But now Adam was saying that with the baby coming, it was going to be too much—us, the baby, and a dog all in one room together. I tried to convince him it was Bohemian. I tried to appeal to his pretensions. But he was unbending. Last month we did a dry run, putting Lucy to sleep in the living room. I listened to her all night as she alternated between quietly whimpering and frantically scraping at the door. *She has to learn*, Adam kept saying. *She has to learn*. But she was seven, or forty-nine, or close enough to it, and she had become who she had become. For better or worse. Finally, at four in the morning, I let her into the room and lied down next to her. *Get in bed*, Adam said. I told him I was fine. And I stayed next to Lucy, curled up on her bed until the sun came up.

Adam hadn't been happy with me then and he wasn't happy with me now. He was back in the kitchen, pouring another glass of wine.

"You want your own?" he said, holding up the bottle and looking at me.

"Yours tastes better." I smiled at him, hoping to smooth things over.

He handed his glass to me and held on to it even when my hand was on the stem.

"I don't want to fight," he said, letting the glass go.

"Neither do I."

"She's too dependent on you."

"It's not her fault." For years, it had just been the two of us, Lucy and me. We were dependent on each other. It was the first time I had experienced unconditional love. Adam was the second. Not second best, just next chronologically.

"She's going to lose it when the baby comes," he said.

"She'll be fine."

"You don't know that." His voice was quiet, almost a whisper. Maybe he didn't want to give Lucy any ideas.

"Okay, Adam, you're right. She's ferocious. A killer. She'll maul the baby. Is that what you think?"

"That's a nice thing to joke about. Mauled babies. Hilarious."

"You know what? Fuck you."

Adam looked at me and shook his head, as if he was disappointed, although not entirely surprised. He thought I had anger management issues. He said I cursed too much and spoke too little. I had a habit of shutting down. But fighting with him could be maddening, the way he always played the part of the cool, rational one. Like a therapist, his voice becoming soft and steady, full of condescension. *Are you sure that's what you believe? Can you say more about what you're feeling? Do you really want to know what I think?*

Right now, as we stood across from each other in the kitchen with Lucy at my side, I knew exactly what he was thinking. Him or the dog? He wanted to know where my loyalties lay. With him or her? If push came to shove, which one would I choose? Or maybe he thought I had already chosen. Maybe he thought keeping Lucy was an affront to him. But I had been with Lucy longer. She had that on him. Yes, Adam was my lover, the father of my child-to-be, but Lucy was my companion, my best friend. She knew I was pregnant before I did. She became more protective. They say that dogs can tell. They have a sixth sense. We could all use one of those.

Lucy was the first one to hear Paul's car pull into the driveway. She was at the door, her bark moving into a lower, throatier range, the bark she reserved for strangers. It belied how friendly and harmless she truly was. I followed her and Adam followed me.

"Let the games begin," he said.

I tried to shush Lucy. "It's Paul," I said. "Lucy, it's Paul. Are you excited? Yes, you are. Yes, you are. I know you are."

"I'm excited too," Adam said. "Yes, I am. Yes, I am."

I looked at him and rolled my eyes. I wasn't in the mood.

Once Paul was inside, he set his hands on either side of my stomach. "Wow," he said. "It's real."

"It's real," I said. Paul hadn't aged much since I last saw him almost three years ago. His hair was thinner, as was his face, his cheekbones and jawline more pronounced, but he still looked like him. Confident and manly, but not unkind. Professorial with his glasses. He bent down and brought Lucy's face to his. "Hey, Lucy-loo. You remember me? You remember Paul?"

The three of us—me, Adam, and Paul's good friend—went about our introductions while Paul and Lucy got reacquainted.

"I'm Masha," Paul's friend said. She was about my height and blonde, like me, but younger. The newer model.

Paul stood up and pulled a bottle of wine out of a paper bag. "For you," he said, handing it to me. And then he reached back into the bag and displayed a bone, the meat and gristle still tethered to it. It must have been the leg of a small animal, a lamb or a pig. A calf.

"And for you," Paul said, presenting the bone to Lucy, who jumped onto his legs, resting her front paws on his thighs.

"I hope it's okay," Paul said.

"Of course," I said. Lucy held the big bone awkwardly in her mouth and trotted off to the living room.

"Should keep her busy for about five minutes," Adam said.

"Adam's not really a dog person," I fake-whispered to Paul. Later, Adam would bring this up. In bed, he would ask me why I had said that, why I felt the need to disparage him in front of Paul. I hadn't meant to be disparaging. I was only telling the truth.

We eventually migrated into the living room, where Lucy

was already under the coffee table. Masha and Paul sat side by side on the love seat, where Adam and I had earlier failed to make love. We both claimed a chair now on opposite sides of the table, where I had set out the plate of the miniquiches and the cutting board.

"To you two," Paul said, raising a glass of wine. "You three," he corrected himself, gesturing at my belly. We all clinked our glasses and sipped our wine.

"Do you know what you're having?" Masha asked with more enthusiasm than seemed natural. She was overdressed for the occasion, and I noticed her frequently tugging at her strapless top that slid easily down her flat, tan chest. Paul and Adam were in jeans, and I had on flip-flops and a cotton jersey dress, one that accommodated my ever-expanding girth.

"We want it to be a surprise," I said, reflexively setting a hand on my belly, as if to guard what was inside. The men had angled their bodies to face each other while Masha and I did the same, so that our knees were practically touching. It was boys on one side, girls on the other.

"I could never do that," she said. "I'm too much of a planner."

There always seemed to be a bit of judgment in people's voices when they said this. Like we would be wholly unprepared for the baby simply because its sex had not been revealed to us.

"Well, we thought it would be nice to be surprised," I said.

"Oh, absolutely," she said. "I just feel like life has so many surprises. The more I know, the better."

"To each his own," I said.

She smiled and raised her glass in my direction, as if to congratulate my aberrant decision. "I have a niece and nephew," she said, swallowing her wine.

I nodded and reached for a miniquiche, placing the whole thing in my mouth.

"It's not the same, I know," she said. "But aunthood is as close as I can get to motherhood. At least for now."

"What do you do?" I asked, cupping my hand over my mouth as I chewed.

"I'm in finance," Masha said, pronouncing the word with a short i, an accent on the second syllable.

"Like Paul," I said.

"Sort of. Paul works in futures. I'm in swaps."

"I see," I said, smiling. I was trying to be polite, to keep the conversation alive. Paul had already given me a rundown on Masha's credentials. She was from New Jersey and had gone to Duke and then Wharton, she was twenty-nine, she lived downtown, and worked at one of the big banks, something exotic-sounding like Deutsche or Credit Suisse. They had met on a blind date. That was three months ago.

"It's boring," she said.

I nodded because I believed her. What she did was boring. Important, sure, but still boring as hell. I never even had understood what Paul did, something about arbitrage, which sounded both dangerous and illegal, but was actually neither.

"So what do you do?" she asked.

I had slipped off my shoe and was curling my toes against Lucy's back as she lay under the table, still gnawing at her bone.

"I'm a producer," I said.

"She's amazing," Paul said, looking over his shoulder. "Ask her what she's done."

"Please don't," I said. "It's nothing anyone would have seen."

"Try me," Masha said.

"*Jews in Green?*"

Masha shook her head apologetically, not that she had anything to be sorry for. It was a documentary about Jews in the U.S. military. It had premiered at a film festival in Fort Lauderdale.

"What else?" she asked.

"Mostly documentaries. Small-release stuff."

"Did you see the one about fast food?"

"*Super Size Me,*" I said.

93

"Yes!" she said, clapping her hands and falling back on the couch, kicking up a slender leg.

"Yeah. That's not mine." I smiled and poured more wine for Masha and myself. I overheard Paul and Adam resume their conversation about tennis. Federer versus Nadal. Clay courts versus grass. Strength versus grace. Men always had sports to fall back on. Their universal language. Women, if they had kids, could talk about that, about schools and first words and organic foods; otherwise, we were at a loss.

"So," I said. "Does Paul still put his trash in the refrigerator?"

"Yes," Masha said, leaning in excitedly.

"It's exclusively food-related trash," Paul said, chiming in. "I don't want bugs."

"Right," I said, remembering the plastic wrappers and cardboard containers he would store in his refrigerator until he took out the garbage.

"What?" he said.

"It's a little crazy," I said.

"Can you two try not to gang up on me?" Paul asked, but I knew he was flattered, that the two of us were getting along, were bonding over him.

"Memories," Adam sang. "Light the corners of my mind."

"And the white noise?" Masha said, referring to the machine Paul used to fall asleep. She made the sound now, like a bad connection on a cell phone. Lucy perked up, cocking her head to the side.

"And talking in his sleep," I said. This was turning out to be sort of fun.

Masha sprung to her feet, imitating Paul. "Buy, buy! Sell, sell!" she screamed with her eyes closed. Startled, Lucy stood up quickly, too quickly, forgetting she was under the table. Two glasses of wine wobbled, then fell, first on the table and then onto the floor.

"Lucy!" Adam yelled, yanking her by the collar.

"It was an accident," I said.

"Oh God, it's totally my fault," Masha said. "I'm so sorry." She was reaching for the cocktail napkins, trying to soak up the red wine. The glasses had shattered and thin shards twinkled in the dim light of the room.

"Come here, Lucy," I said, trying to steer her away from the mess. She lumbered over to me with her tail between her legs. "Paul, can you take her while I clean this up?"

"Let me help you," Masha said, standing up.

"No, no. Sit. It's fine."

I squatted carefully, the way I'd been taught in yoga for mommies-to-be, and picked up the big pieces of glass. Adam was next to me, also squatting.

"I can do that," he said.

"Keep Masha company." I carried a handful of glass into the kitchen, with Lucy and Paul trailing close behind.

"Masha seems nice," I said once we were safely out of earshot. I held out the broken pieces of glass in my hand. "Do you think I can recycle this?"

"Why not?" Paul said.

"She's young."

"She's twenty-nine. There was a time when we would have thought that was old."

"Don't remind me."

"Adam, he's a good one."

"Yeah," I said. "He is." I had been waiting for a good one, someone like Adam who wanted the things I wanted: stability, comfort, babies.

"Not Lucy's biggest fan."

I sensed this was my opportunity. "Paul?" I said.

"Erin?" he said, mimicking my grave tone.

"She adores you."

"Masha?" He sounded surprised.

"Lucy."

"Well, in that case, the feeling is mutual." He scratched her behind her ear as she leaned in affectionately.

"I want you to have her," I said.

"Whoa," he said, taking a step away.

I told him that I had thought about it, and I truly believed this was the best thing. For Lucy. For us. It wasn't a hard case to make. "We're going to have our hands full once the baby comes," I said. As it was, Lucy had already started acting out, having accidents and chasing her own tail. The vet said she had anxiety and displacement issues. He suggested Prozac. Lucy on Prozac. The very idea of it seemed wrong.

"What does Adam think?" Paul asked.

"It's not really his decision."

"So he doesn't know?"

"He'll be relieved."

Paul nodded solemnly, his face serious, as if he were doing a complicated equation in his head. Adding and subtracting. Carrying the one. When he finally made eye contact with me, I waved a hand in front of my face as I felt the tears take shape.

"Hormones," I said.

"I can't," he said. "I'm sorry."

"Yes, you can."

"I'm working twelve-hour days and traveling."

"You could get a dog-sitter."

"She's your dog."

"You were always her favorite." Lucy was in between us now, looking back and forth as we each spoke, as though hanging on our every word, as if she knew we were discussing her fate.

"I wish I could," he said.

I took a deep breath and grabbed some dish towels.

"So that's it?" he said.

"Can you get the broom?" I pointed in the direction of the closet. "The dustpan should be there too."

"Don't be mad," he said. "If it's too much, I'll help you. We'll find a good home for her. Someplace not so far away."

"Forget it," I said.

We walked back into the living room and Adam and Masha, who had claimed the two surviving wineglasses, looked up at us.

"Welcome back, compadres," Adam said.

"What did we miss?" I asked.

"How it would only be fair for Masha and I to sleep together," he said. "Just to even the score."

Masha looked embarrassed. "We were joking," she said, looking at me. "We were saying that you and I have already slept together since we both slept with Paul."

I raised my eyebrows. "I see."

"This isn't translating well," Masha said.

"No. I get it," I said, playing along. "Or Masha, you could *actually* sleep with me. That would also work. Because then you and Adam will have slept together by proxy."

"Right," Masha said. "Exactly."

"Or I could sleep with Paul," Adam said, winking at no one in particular. He was definitely a little too drunk. Maybe we all were.

Lucy had gone over to Masha now, who was picking at the plate of cheese. She rested her face in Masha's lap and drooled on her white pants.

"She's such a sweetheart," Masha said, crossing her legs and scooching away.

"Do you want a dog?" I asked wryly.

"I have a cat," she said.

"So you're a cat person," I said. It was more of an observation than an insult, but Paul quickly came to her defense.

"Her cat's got a lot of personality," he said.

"A pussy with personality," Adam said, under his breath but loud enough for us all to hear.

"Someone's cut off," I said.

"Who?" Adam said. He announced that he was going to get some fresh air, which was code for going to smoke, and Paul volunteered to join him. Maybe so they could have some man-time. A heart-to-heart. Or maybe because Paul really did need fresh air. It was a cool Southern California night with a hazy lavender sky.

"Cinderella?" Paul said, looking to Masha, handing her the broom and dustpan so we could sweep up the remaining slivers of glass.

"Take Lucy," I said. "She might have to go."

"C'mon, Lulu." Paul patted his thigh and he guided Lucy into the backyard after Adam.

"You're a good sport," Masha said once we were the only ones left in the living room. She swept the glass into a pile while I used the damp towels to sop up the wine.

"I try," I said.

"I don't know if I could do it," she said with a mix of admiration and pity, the way you might speak about an overworked mother.

"Do what?"

"You seem so calm," she said. "With everything." She waved her hand around, gesturing at our sparsely decorated Ikea living room, at the mess on the floor, at the men outside.

I smiled and shrugged. "I embrace chaos," I said, and Masha nodded as if this was something knowing and profound.

"How come it didn't work?" she asked. "Between you and Paul?" I could tell she was looking for some kind of reassurance, the baby I was having with another man not convincing enough.

"We were young," I said, realizing that even then, we were older than Masha was now.

"He talks about you a lot," she said.

"He and I were meant to be great friends."

"And Adam doesn't mind?"

"That we're friends?"

"Well, *great* friends," she said, monitoring my every word.

"Adam and I both have our own histories. When you get to be a certain age, you expect that. People have *great* friends."

"I must sound so naive."

"Look," I said. "Paul and I were both looking for something more than what we had with each other. That's all."

She seemed satisfied with that response, or at least enough so that she didn't ask any more questions.

Paul and Adam came back in with Lucy proudly wagging her tail, walking between them.

"Did she go?" I asked.

"Yes, it is a lovely night outside," Adam said. "Thank you for asking."

"She went," Paul said. "Number one."

"Good girl, Lucy," I said. I took a piece of salami off the plate and she came over, sitting obediently.

"What do I get when I pee?" Adam asked.

"You can have salami too," I said.

Adam put up his hand to high five Paul, who was mouthing something to Masha and didn't notice the gesture.

"Don't leave me hanging," Adam said, which sounded ridiculous coming from him. Or coming from anyone for that matter.

We left the pile of glass at the foot of the sofa, under an end table, along with a clump of soggy paper towels.

"I'll deal with it later," I said, calling Lucy over so she was on the couch beside me.

The seating arrangement had been modified. Adam was in one chair, and Paul and Masha shared the other, with Masha sitting on the armrest, leaning against Paul. Someone, probably Adam, had brought out the Scotch and everyone except for me was sipping it. I stuck with wine. It felt less egregious.

"Smoky," Masha said, which was what you always said about Scotch when you had nothing to say about it.

As the night wore on, we regressed. We curled our tongues and bent our double-jointed fingers and thumbs. Masha raised one eyebrow, and Paul named the capitals of Pennsylvania and Kentucky and South Dakota, which no one else could do.

It made sense then that the night would end up the way it did. We weren't young. We weren't in college or just out of college. We were grown-ups. Adults with retirement funds and mortgages and master's degrees. We might have been embarrassed by our behavior if we weren't so tipsy and ironic, playing the game as if it was all one big joke.

I think it was Paul who went first, who said something like, "Never have I ever had sex in public," and we all drank, because that's the way we played the game: you drank if you were guilty, and we loved to incriminate ourselves. Masha was in his lap now, sitting sideways, her long legs draped over the side of the chair.

"Never have I ever," she said, pausing for a moment to think, "kissed a woman."

"Amateur," Adam said, and he drank along with the rest of us. I rested my head against Lucy, who was asleep at one end of the couch. She yawned and stretched.

"Never have I ever had an orgy," Adam said, and waited. Nobody drank except for him.

"Nice," Paul said, raising his glass to Adam.

Adam had told me all about his orgy, a drug-induced college night, him and four other people, after hours of studying. They all took ecstasy and waited to feel ecstatic.

"Your turn, Erin," Masha said. She was excited to hear what I had to offer.

"Never have I ever," I said, and I thought about what came next: never have I ever masturbated at work or been taped having sex—something Adam was keen on. The thing about the game was that we all wanted to say things that we had done, things we desperately needed to reveal to others, to shock and surprise and impress. Every statement had a story behind it, something people were waiting to confess.

Adam nudged me gently on the shoulder with his foot.

"Never have I ever," I began again, "been unfaithful to some-one I love."

"Define unfaithful," Adam said.

"Define someone you love," Paul said.

I closed my eyes for a moment and buried my face in Lucy's coat, which smelled musty and salty like an old beach blanket. It was a smell I hoped I would be able to remember forever.

"Use your own judgment," I told them.

And everyone drank.

neither here nor there

First and foremost, this is a ghost story, although I'm not a man who typically believes in ghosts. For more than twenty-six years, there has been one living in my home. The ghost is my son who was born dying, with an umbilical cord, thick and tough as a garden hose, wrapped around his flimsy neck.

For my wife, Lydia, it was easier to pretend this son never existed. His death was a betrayal by her body, which had always been small and strong, full of power, kinetic energy. She had trusted it wholeheartedly, put her faith in its details, in her blood pressure and hormone levels and the circumference of her belly, all of which were normal.

The baby lived for almost twenty-four hours. Doctors threaded small tubes through his nose and inserted needles in his frail veins. The social worker recommended that we save a photograph of the baby. She offered to take the picture herself, a picture of us cradling this cold, nearly weightless body. She suggested that we give him a name. It would help us grieve. The rabbi said a name was necessary to help us find him in heaven. But Lydia wasn't interested. She had stopped believing in heaven. Besides, she didn't want help grieving. To mourn the loss was to say her body had in some way failed. That the baby was even a boy, that he was real enough to have a gender, was too much for her to bear.

It was not in my nature to defy my wife. If she told me I didn't like my bagel toasted, I didn't like it toasted. If she told me I'd had enough to drink, I stopped drinking. What she said, went.

But not this time.

I gave our baby a name. Jacob. After my grandfather, my father's father. It was a name I whispered to myself at night, to make sure I never forgot.

A year later, Lydia gave birth to Emily, healthy and pink, ten fingers and ten toes. When Emily was four, she had an imaginary friend.

"Who are you talking to?" I once asked her. She was sitting on the floor in her bedroom, whispering and giggling, picking up oversized puzzle pieces and turning them around in her hands.

"Jacob," she said, too preoccupied with her puzzle to look at me.

"Who's Jacob?" I asked, trying to hold the sound of my voice steady.

"A little boy," she said, as if this was the most obvious thing in the world.

Before bed, Emily might say to me, "Jacob wants you to read him a story." It was always one of the books about the bears in the tree house. *The Berenstain Bears.* I called them the Bernstein Bears. (They're not Jewish, Lydia used to say.)

In the mornings, Jacob would sit next to Emily at breakfast. We had to pour him cereal—half Cheerios and half Rice Krispies. That was the way he liked it, according to Emily. Lydia said it was normal, perfectly healthy even, for children to have imaginary friends. She had read the books on parenting and taken notes in the margins. According to Lydia, imaginary friends were a sign of intelligence. Emily, she said, was testing the boundary between fantasy and reality; it was a phase she would outgrow in time.

Sure enough, Lydia was right. One morning at breakfast I put down an extra cereal bowl.

"Who's that for?" Emily asked.

"Jacob," I said.

"Oh," she said. "He's died."

"Dead?" I asked.

She nodded knowingly, her little-girl face pinched and grave.

"How did Jacob die?" I asked.

"He just did," Emily said. She held out the bowl for me to take.

"Are you sad?" I asked her.

She thought for a moment and said, "It's okay."

We buried Jacob, the real Jacob, at the cemetery where I work. I was a salesman, a broker of final resting places. I worked on commission. If you wanted to be under a tree or alongside your wife or as far from her as possible, I was your man. You locked in a price when you purchased your spot; whether you died tomorrow or in ten years, you got the same deal.

We waived the burial fees for babies. You just paid for the plot of land. Jacob's gravestone said "Baby Krauss, June 2, 1979." I visited him every year on his birthday, his only day, which Lydia never acknowledged. I used to try to be kinder to her on that day, to make her coffee and be sure to kiss her good-bye. But eventually I realized there was no point.

You might think after Emily's imaginary friend disappeared, that would have been the end of Jacob, but it wasn't. I saw him every now and again. When my mother passed away, he was at the funeral. When Emily graduated from high school, I swear on my life I saw him in the crowd. When I accidentally backed the lawn mower over my foot, grinding two toes into a mushy pulp like fruit in a blender, he was at the hospital. Lydia would have said it was the painkillers, but I could have sworn I saw him walk by my room, pausing for a moment to check in on me.

He was always lingering in the background, taking it all in. He was just out of reach, disappearing as soon as I worked up the nerve to say something. Over the years he changed, his hair growing darker and thicker, his jaw strengthening, becoming square and muscled. He had Lydia's coloring, skin the sun loved, and almost-black eyes that shimmered like puddles of gasoline.

In the meantime, Emily grew up too. She got married and then divorced, all before her twenty-fifth birthday. She started dating women and announced she was a bisexual. I said she was a hedonist, but for Lydia it was a point of pride. Having a bisexual daughter made her seem worldy and modern. Not that I was against it. I just thought it was ridiculous. Choose a team.

But everything happens for a reason. Emily met a girl named Isabelle, and Lydia invited them over for dinner. She was making red trout, like salmon but a little fancier, and the whole house smelled of fish, all the way into our bedroom, where I was getting dressed. Lydia had laid out an outfit for me on the bed, a yellow cable-knit sweater and khaki pants. She'd said it was a summer sweater, whatever that meant. My leather loafers were placed on the carpet at the pants' cuffs. It looked as though a man had disappeared, vanished into thin air, leaving his empty clothes behind.

"Can you get that?" Lydia yelled when the doorbell rang.

It was Emily and Isabelle, both of them wearing ripped jeans that looked two sizes too big, along with flimsy tank tops and sandals. Their hair was pulled back into high, swingy ponytails and they were holding hands. They looked like best friends, not whatever it was they actually were.

During dinner, Lydia let loose, drinking wine and toasting to this and that: to new beginnings, to new friends, to summer coming, to making this a tradition, and so on and so forth. Her hair came slightly undone, the straight silver strands usually tucked behind her ear falling over a single eye. Even at fifty-two, Lydia was still pretty enough to wear her hair long, all the way to her shoulders.

"So what exactly do you do, Isabelle?" she asked.

"I'm an artist."

"Lovely! What sort of artist are you?"

"A painter."

"She has a gallery in Venice," Emily said. She rubbed her shoulders as if she was cold, which she may have been, so barely dressed and all.

"Italy?" I asked, getting up to adjust the temperature of the AC.

"California," Emily said. The Venice in California is only some twenty miles from us on the 405. It's got canals, but that's about as close as it gets to Italy.

"What do you paint?" Lydia asked, leaning in, resting her sharp elbows on the table.

"It's hard to explain," Isabelle said.

"It's like Kandinsky," Emily said. "But not derivative." When had my daughter become smarter than me? You could put a pistol to my head and I still wouldn't be able to tell you who Kandinsky was.

"They're more Kandinsky-like than like Kandinsky," Isabelle said. She looked at me and I nodded as though this all made perfect sense.

"His paintings were improvisation, just what came to him," she said. "That's how painting is for me. Whatever comes, whatever I see. Images, words, colors. It's the only way I know to get them out of my head."

She picked a piece of asparagus off Emily's plate and took a bite. "I know it sounds crazy," she said.

"No it doesn't," Emily said. "Her paintings are psychic." She looked at her mother and me as she said this.

"So you paint the future," Lydia said. "That's wonderful."

"Sort of," Isabelle said. "It's hard to explain."

"How interesting," Lydia said.

"I have always been very aware of the energy around us," Isabelle explained. "Ever since I was little." She told us she sensed Emily had what she called sensitive powers too.

"I think she gets it from you," she said.

"Me?" I said, looking directtly at me.

Lydia laughed into her hand and glanced at Emily, who widened her eyes and shrugged as if to say, anything's possible.

"It's just a feeling I get," Isabelle said.

Before she and Emily left, Lydia corralled us all into a game of Scrabble. Even tipsy, she managed to win. Isabelle kept making up words that she said should be words and Emily said I was no fun when I spelled simple words like "cat" and "top."

When they left, Isabelle wrapped her thin, pale arms around me and held on tight.

"It was really nice to meet you," she said.

I smiled clownishly, the corners of my mouth curling up, my lips pressed together. I'm pretty sure I was blushing like an old fool.

"Bye, Daddy," Emily said, kissing me lightly on the cheek. The girls walked away. They were holding hands, swinging their arms back and forth.

That night, Lydia teased me about being sensitive. She made little quotation marks with her fingers when she said the word.

"You're so 'sensitive,'" she said. "Just wait until this girl sees you hungry."

This was the joke in my family: when I was hungry, I got mean and grouchy. It was true; I was a man who needed to eat often. I kept granola bars and bags of peanuts in my pockets.

"Mr. Sensitive," Lydia said. "How about you turn off the lights so I can go to sleep."

I closed the book that was on my chest and kissed Lydia's warm forehead. She drifted off easily, still under the spell of the wine. But not me. I wondered about what Isabelle had said. I didn't even really know what it meant to be sensitive. I couldn't see the future. In fact, I seemed to see the opposite of the future. I was a man who lived in the past.

After a while of tossing and turning, of Lydia nudging me, I got up and went into our closet. It was a walk-in with plenty of room. The walls were cedar and had a warm, comforting smell, like the woods. Like a camping trip I never took my son on. We would have worn flannel shirts and we would have fished. We would have made a fire and had marshmallows and hot chocolate for dinner. I would say, don't tell your mother.

There was nothing Emily told me that I couldn't tell Lydia. We had no secrets together. I didn't know what information Lydia had about our daughter that I didn't have, the boys she had kissed, or the girls she has kissed, for that matter, the people who had broken her heart, the reasons she married her husband and left him. In my family, I was used to being the outsider; I was the one always outnumbered.

At work the next day, I sold a plot to a young couple who had just gotten married. They wanted to make sure they had a place together, side by side underground, which was something only the newlyweds worried about. The longer you were married, the less tempting it became to be side by side for all eternity.

I told the couple these plots were nonrefundable, although they were transferable.

"Why would you transfer?" the man wanted to know.

"Marriages don't always work," I said. "We have to be prac-tical."

The man nodded. He was wearing a pink shirt and kept his arm around his wife the whole time. She asked me if she could still be buried here if she got a tattoo.

"You're getting a tattoo?" the man said.

"I don't know. But I want to know I'll be able to. Just in case."

I assured her that we had no prohibition against tattoos. That was a myth, a misinterpretation of something in the Bible.

"What would you get?" the man asked.

"I don't know. A dandelion. Or a feather."

I saw him roll his eyes, but I think the wife missed it. We rode a golf cart around the grounds, looking at what was avail-able. The couple was picky, which I didn't begrudge them. Final resting places are no small thing. We went by the children's gar-den, where Jacob was buried. His final resting place. Nowhere near his parents. I had an urge to dig him up, to plunge my hands into the dirt and scoop him out.

"You got a license to drive this thing?" the man said, sitting next to me.

"Sorry," I said, slowing down.

I called Emily that afternoon from my office. "Your friend was nice," I said.

"She's not my friend, Dad. She's my *girlfriend*."

"Well, she was nice."

"Thanks."

"Do you think I'm sensitive?" I asked her.

"Isabelle reads people really well."

"Em?" I said.

"Yeah."

"Do you remember when you had an imaginary friend?"

"I did?"

"His name was Jacob," I said.

"Daddy, I'm sort of busy right now."

"Is Isabelle with you?"

"Yes," she said.

I asked if I could speak to her. From one sensitive person to another, I said, laughing a little, trying to make light of the whole matter.

"Seriously?" Emily asked.

"Seriously," I said.

"Okay," Emily said. "Just don't embarrass me." I heard her yell, "Belly, phone!" and then Isabelle picked up.

"It's Emily's father," I said.

"Hello, Emily's father," she said.

"Hello," I said.

There was a pause.

"What's on your mind?" she asked me.

"This and that. Do you know?"

She laughed. "No," she said. "I'm not a mind reader." I heard Emily in the background. "Jesus, Dad," she said.

I apologized. "I'm just trying to understand this," I said.

"Why don't you come by the gallery?"

I protested at first, but then relented.

"Cool," she said.

That night I asked Lydia if she believed in Isabelle's psychic paintings.

"I believe that she believes in it. And I believe that Emily believes in it. What I think is neither here nor there."

Neither here nor there was Lydia's catchall phrase for things she could not make sense of, things that didn't fit neatly into her way of seeing the world. Instead of arguing, she decided things mattered so little that they were neither here nor there. Of no consequence at all.

During my lunch break the next day I stopped to pick up two corned beef sandwiches, salty, fatty meat that Lydia wouldn't let me eat on account of my cholesterol. This was how she showed she cared. She kept me alive.

I drove to Isabelle's gallery in Venice. It was only a few miles from the cemetery. As I got closer to the beach, the air changed. It was June gloom around here, when the fog sat on the beach until late in the afternoon: Only then would the sun come out, as though everyone had finally earned it.

It made sense that Isabelle would live out here. In my day, we would have called her a hippie. All free-spirited and loving—not that this was a bad way to be. Isabelle opened the door wearing overalls and no shoes. There was paint on her feet, in between her toes. She greeted me with a hug, the same hug she had given when she left our home.

"Emily doesn't know how to hug either," she said to me. She took my hand like Emily used to do when we crossed the street or walked through a crowd, holding on to just the fingers, except that now I felt like the child. I didn't know what I expected to find here. More reassurance that I was sensitive?

But I followed her through the gallery, stepping over paint cans and kicking aside empty bottles of water. Canvases, works in progress, you could say, leaned against the walls on either side of us. I read the cursive black letters that had been painted on one big white wall: "The most fundamental reason one paints is in order to see."

"I love that," Isabelle said, following my eyes and smiling.

"You wrote it?"

"I mean I wrote it on the wall, but I didn't come up with it."
She handed me a paintbrush.

"No thanks," I said.

"People are afraid to paint. They overthink it. It's not like singing. It's not like you're going to hit the wrong note."

"I can't sing either," I said. "Completely tone-deaf." I opened the brown paper bag and held it out, the smell of corned beef and pickles resting heavily in the space between us. "Sandwich?" I said.

"I can't eat when I'm working." I wondered if, with her long, skinny arms, she was ever not working.

"Do you mind?" I asked, holding up one of my neatly wrapped sandwiches.

"Be my guest."

I looked at the half-finished paintings with sharp lines and bold colors overlapping each other, all vying for space. Some of them had writing on them, words like "battle" or "electric" or "firmament."

"Note to self," I said, holding up my index finger. "Look up 'firmament.'"

"It's what divides heaven from earth."

"No kidding."

"This one," she said, pointing to the painting with "electric" on it, "this was bought by a woman who was trying to decide whether or not to buy a house on Electric Avenue."

"So she bought it?"

Isabelle nodded.

"And does this mean an earthquake is coming?" I asked, gesturing with my corned beef sandwich to one of the paintings that had the word "earthquake" written across the canvas.

"I hope not," she said. She explained to me that the paintings weren't always literal. It could just mean that someone's world was going to be shaken up. I considered how this could apply to anyone. What was so psychic about that?

Then she reached behind one of the canvases on the floor

and brought out another painting. "I just finished this one," she told me.

I felt the strands of hair on my neck go stiff. I felt both terrified and excited. I was still clutching my corned beef sandwich in one hand while I touched the canvas with the other, running my fingers over the paint.

"Who is it?" I asked.

"I don't know."

"Have you seen him?"

"Not until I painted him."

It was unmistakably my son, his same dark eyes and square jaw that I had come to recognize in my visions. I thought about the possibilities. Perhaps it was Emily's face that Isabelle had painted, a version of it, hardened and more masculine. Or maybe both Isabelle and I had conjured up the same generic face, one nondescript enough that anyone might have been able to claim him as someone they knew.

I know that most things can be explained logically. I know there's a 1 in 200 chance you'll board a train and meet someone you know. I know a monkey hitting keys at random on a typewriter for an infinite amount of time will almost surely write *Moby-Dick*.

But when you put it all together, it was impossible not to believe it meant something.

"How much do you want for it?" I asked.

Isabelle told me she couldn't take my money. She claimed I was like family, but I insisted.

"I'll miss this one," she said, touching Jacob's face gently as if brushing away a stray crumb. We hugged good-bye and she whispered, "You're getting better."

Lydia was on the couch watching CNN when I got home. I stood in front of the TV with the painting.

"You make a better door than a window, dear."

"Do you know who this is?"

"I have no idea," she said, getting up from the couch. "I'm going to heat up leftovers. Is that fine for you?"

"Look at it, Lydia. Look at the painting."

"What?" she said. "I'm looking. Is he an actor? Should I know him? I'm terrible with faces."

I held out the painting so her face was even with Jacob's.

"This is your son, Lydia. Don't you recognize him?"

"What are you talking about?" she said, shooing the painting away and walking toward the kitchen.

"Your son," I yelled.

"You're crazy," she said from the kitchen, her voice barely raised enough for me to hear, almost as if she was saying it only to herself, as if I was already a lost cause.

Maybe she was right. I was sixty-four, old enough to start losing my mind, for those little perforations to start forming in my brain. I took the painting with me to the bedroom and placed it in the cedar closet.

Neither of us brought it up during dinner. Except for the occasional slurping of spaghetti, we were practically silent. Lydia hummed a bit in between bites, but I just focused on the plate in front of me.

"There's one meatball left," Lydia said, dragging a spoon through the pot. They were turkey meatballs.

"You have it," I said.

"I don't want it."

"I'll take it, then."

She served the meatball and watched as I ate it.

"You wouldn't know it's turkey," she said with pride.

"I would," I said.

"Well, you're a man of very refined taste."

She smiled and I didn't say anything. I calmly set down my fork and looked at her.

"For the record," I said. "We did have a son."

Lydia pushed her chair back and stood up. "Are you done?" she asked, reaching for my plate.

"His name was Jacob," I said as she left the room. If nothing else, Lydia would be able to find him in heaven.

the last ice age

Only a few weeks after my divorce is finally final, I go back in time. Back before his affair and before mine. Before getting married and falling in love. Before I even met the man I no longer knew.

"At the tar pits," I say to my students, "you'll get a sense of what Los Angeles was like between ten thousand and forty thousand years ago, during the last Ice Age, when saber-toothed cats and wooly mammoths roamed the area. Who can tell me why the number of predators preserved outnumber the prey?"

We are on the school bus, lumbering down Wilshire Boulevard, being passed by the impatient cars around us.

Reagan is the only girl to raise her hand, not eagerly but in a halfhearted way, her elbow resting on the seat in front of her, her wrist flung to the side. As if this whole process of waiting to be called on is beneath her.

"Liz," she says. "Question."

My class calls me by my first name because I've told them to. I have even given them my phone number in case of an emergency. So far, I've gotten a few hang-ups, a couple heavy breathers, and the occasional fart.

"Do we get a lunch break?" Reagan wants to know. The girls

have brought their own lunches, prepackaged sushi or dense cookies, individually wrapped. The cookie alone is the meal. The Cookie Diet. The few who are not lactose-intolerant eat cottage cheese. They all want to be thin and pale and date vampires, beautiful boys who will kill you if they fall too much in love.

I tell Reagan that lunch is from one thirty to two. Her eyes roll back. For a moment, you only see the whites of them. She mumbles something about low blood sugar. Next time she will bring a doctor's note.

The other girls sigh loudly in a show of solidarity. They cross their arms and shake their heads at the injustice. Avery stage-whispers that the bus ride is going to be the best part of the trip. Avery is part of Reagan's inner circle. She and Campbell have made the cut. Avery, Campbell, and Reagan. Where have all the Jessicas and Heathers and Jennifers gone?

I've lost my audience. If they remember that I asked them a question, they don't show it. Instead, Reagan suggests they play a game. The girls call it "Either Or." They debate whether they'd rather marry a blind man or one in a wheelchair.

"Is he a paraplegic or a quadriplegic?" Reagan asks. She is taking the question into serious consideration, weighing the options.

I already know what my answer would be.

"Paraplegic, I guess," Campbell says. She sucks on the end of her hair, shaping it into a fine tip.

"Then him. For sure."

"Okay, paraplegic or obese?"

"I wouldn't marry someone obese," Reagan says.

"But if you were in love with him."

"I wouldn't be," she says. "No offense."

Who is she worried about offending?

The next round begins: "A finger or a boob? Which would you rather have cut off?"

The details are hammered out. You are under anesthesia. It is your pointer finger, all of it, right down to the knuckle. Pick a hand, any hand. Pick a breast. Right or left. It's not important. (But of course, it is.) You can have reconstructive surgery. On the breast, not the finger. You won't feel any pain.

The trip to the Rancho La Brea Tar Pits is part of the curriculum at Hampton Hills Academy. I only started teaching here after my husband left. I needed an outlet. I needed an income. It was easier to get hired in Beverly Hills, at a private school, than in Watts. You don't even need a master's degree, although they take your fingerprints. You can't be too safe.

The girls' game continues. They raise the stakes. Have sex with either another woman or an eighty-year-old man.

"Is the other woman pretty?" they want to know.

I look out the window at either just the right time or exactly the wrong time. We are driving by the IHOP, the one where my husband told me he had met someone else.

"I'm in love," my husband had said as I stared down at my pancake with its chocolate chip smile. He wanted me to be happy for him. He said maybe it could be a blessing in disguise. I said it was an awfully good disguise.

We pass a Ralphs, Smart & Final, Baja Fresh, Koo Koo Roo. Then there are the tar pits, a strange, anachronistic hiccup in the landscape, a vast and bubbling pool in the middle of Wilshire Boulevard.

"Are we there yet?" the girls ask.

The natives are getting restless. They would rather be at the mall. Once we get to the museum, they are not impressed. It is a poor man's Disneyland, a cheap ride, with narrow halls and shoddy displays. The girls giggle at the hologram of a bare-breasted prehistoric female. She is only twenty years old. The La Brea Woman. Translation: The The Tar Woman. As if one definite article isn't enough. (I should have taught English.) You can only see her from a certain angle, flesh materializing over bone.

"God, her boobs are saggy," Reagan says.

"Like fried eggs."

"Gross."

"That's what happens when you don't wear a bra," someone says. Could that be true? For years I didn't wear a bra. Nobody did.

The museum guide tells us the woman is around twenty years old. The girls are horrified. They have soft breasts, tender and new.

Nine thousand years ago, being twenty was middle age, the guide says. The elders were in their thirties. This makes me ancient.

The guide lowers her voice, cupping her hand over her mouth. She says the La Brea Woman's death may not have been an accident. She was hit with a blunt instrument before she fell into the tar. A prehistoric murder. Perhaps it was a jealous lover. A romantic rival? As if the saber-toothed cats hadn't been enough to worry about.

There was a dog with the woman when she died. They found canine bones beside her. This consoles me. At least she wasn't alone. Not entirely.

We have lunch outside, sitting on rocks, big, cartoonish boulders. Fred Flintstone comes to mind. One of the girls says, "This is the pits." It's not a bad joke.

They add up their calories, taking small deductions for chewing.

"Spicy foods speed up your metabolism," Avery says.

"Obviously," Reagan says.

Normally I eat lunch in the teacher's lounge, where everyone warms up leftovers in the microwave. Sometimes there is a plate of cookies or an Entenmann's Danish on the counter with a note nearby that says "help yourself." I usually do.

Even from where we sit, you can smell the tar, hot and black, like a freshly paved road. I understand why the animals were drawn to it. It was the prey, the elephants and bison, that went in first. Then came the predators. Jackpot. A meal that couldn't move. Whole packs of them descended on the tar, trapping themselves alongside their intended victims.

The museum has created a scene of an elephant struggling to escape from the tar. I wonder who came up with this, who wanted to tell this story. The elephant's trunk is suspended mid-flail while her baby watches from the shore. It's enough to break your heart.

When my mother was pregnant, she would drive to the gas station—she called it a filling station—because she craved the scent of gasoline the way other women crave pickles. The first time I was pregnant I craved mustard. The second and third time I craved provolone cheese. By the fourth time I didn't crave anything.

I have heard from our friends, the ones we still share like toys, taking turns, that my ex-husband is going to be a father. His wife-to-be is young enough to be his daughter. Or mine. I have done the math. Back at the IHOP, I had made him tell me her age.

"What does it matter?" he said. At least he didn't say that age is just a number. Or a state of mind.

"She's close to thirty," he eventually revealed.

"How close?"

"Closer than she is to twenty," he said.

I told him he was a cliché. He said that was a risk he was willing to take. Such a daredevil.

The girls are playing Either Or again. Either drown or starve to death. They all want to starve. This one's too easy.

Here's a harder one: Either sleep with a husband who is afraid to touch you, who thinks your body is broken, out of service, or sleep with a stranger who has eczema on his hands, a man whose cracked fingers feel like cheap lace against your skin.

Either tell your husband you love him or tell him the truth. That you remember loving him but don't remember exactly why. (Because he could talk to your father about baseball? Because he ironed the sheets?)

Either tell him the truth, the whole truth and nothing but the truth, or keep your secret in a deep, dark place. Coat it with nacre like a grain of sand in an oyster.

Once, we picked pearls together in Solvang. They shucked the oyster right in front of us, prying it open with a knife. My pearl was black. They say that makes it more precious.

I think about the La Brea Woman, the oldest Californian, nine thousand years, who has been put back together and enclosed behind glass. I wonder what she did to deserve this. Which side was she on? The good guys or the bad guys? The predator or the prey?

versailles

The year I turned fourteen and got my braces off and started using Sun-In was the same year my father left for Versailles. Not the palace in France. The apartments in Beverly Hills.

During the six months he lived there, I visited once, a couple weeks after he had moved in. He had called the house on a Thursday and asked me over for that Saturday.

"If you're not too busy," he said.

I wasn't.

My mother drove. She parked in front of Versailles and shut off the engine.

"We can turn around," she said. "Right now. We'll tell him you're sick. Or I'm sick."

"It's not a big deal," I said, looking at the building, chalky and peach, the color of children's aspirin. I reached for my bag in the backseat.

"Did you pack clean underpants?" my mother asked. Did she look for opportunities to say words like "underpants" and "boobies" and "pee-pee," or did they just present themselves?

"No," I told her. "I packed dirty ones."

My mother smiled, her eyes crinkling at the edges.

"What?" I said.

"Nothing," she said, but she was still smiling and there was lipstick on her teeth.

My father left because my mother had fallen in love with someone new, a medical supplies salesman turned guru who led weekend-long seminars at hotels by airports. After the first day of the seminar my mother attended, she announced that she was ready to create an "extraordinary life," one that apparently would be without my father, who didn't "get it."

His absence—the actual fact of his being gone—was not so difficult to get used to. Because in a physical sense, he had never really been there anyway. He slept during the day and worked at night. This had made him feel more like a tenant, some eccentric border, than a father. Our conversations were often formal and clumsy, like two people who had lost touch, trying to get reacquainted.

When I knocked on the door to his new apartment, he said, "Who is it?"

"It's me." He had just buzzed me in from downstairs.

"Don't know a Me," he said.

"Your daughter."

"My daughter?" he said, which might have been funny if it wasn't so close to being true.

"Da-ad," I said, the word coming out as two syllables. It sounded foreign to me, like a word I had just learned, one I wasn't sure how to pronounce or even use correctly.

My father opened the door.

"Hi, hi. Welcome to my humble abode."

His apartment smelled like disinfectant, like a doctor's waiting room. It was clean and glossy, a sharp contrast to my father in his rumpled shirt and baseball hat.

"Sit, sit," he said, leading me to one of the sleek black couches. "What can I get you to drink?"

"Juice?" I said.

He clapped his hands together and went into the open kitchen, where he clattered around a bit, searching for a glass.

"I don't spend much time in the kitchen," he said.

"No rush."

"Aha!" He found a single glass and we agreed to share it.

He opened the refrigerator and peered around the door. "Would you settle for water?" he asked.

"Sure."

My father filled the glass with tap water and brought it over. "After you."

I took a sip and handed the glass back to him. We continued like this for a while, passing the glass back and forth, politely taking turns, neither of us saying a word. It was my father who finally spoke.

"What's new?" he asked.

"Nada."

"Things are good?"

"I guess."

"One to ten?" My father rated everything from one to ten. It was one of the few things I knew about him, that and the fact that he went running in jeans and had learned to count cards in college. He still went to Vegas every now and again to try his luck. Or skill, as he called it. There was no such thing as luck.

"Seven," I said to him.

"Good," he said, rubbing his palms back and forth along his legs. "Seven is not bad. It's not great. But it could be worse, right? It could always be worse. Nobody died." He smiled as if that thought alone warmed him, and we resumed the ritual of passing the water, each of us leaving some for the other, until only a drop was left.

"It's yours," my father said.

"You can have it."

"Going once, going twice? Sold!" He tilted the glass back and waited, letting out a big "aaah" when the water hit his mouth.

"So," he said. "What should we talk about?"

I shrugged.

"Well, what do you and your mother talk about?" he asked.

"Nothing really."

"You don't talk about me?"

I shook my head. Right after he left, my mother told me my father was proof that you can love someone and not like him. She said she felt about my father the way some people must feel about their own children.

"The weather?" he said. "Traffic? Sports?"

"Sorry," I said.

"For what?" he asked.

"I don't know." But I did know. I had a pretty good idea. I was sorry we had absolutely nothing to say to each other, even without my mother around. I was sorry I couldn't be nicer, more consoling, or at least entertaining. I was sorry I wasn't a kid like you see on sitcoms, clever and spunky, more parent than child.

"Who needs another drink?" my father said.

"I'm okay."

The kitchen was open with a granite countertop and black leather bar stools. I watched as my father unscrewed a bottle and refilled his glass with Scotch or bourbon. Possibly rum. He dropped in a couple ice cubes and stirred with his crooked pinky, the one that had been closed in a car door years ago. When I was little, he used to let me try to straighten the finger out.

He quickly downed two glasses before we left for dinner. We took his vintage Mustang, and during the drive my father talked about the car's horsepower. I pressed my face against the cold window.

"I'm boring you," he said.

"No," I said. "It's fine." I didn't mind the sound of his voice, slow and more relaxed now, the words coming easily, as if these were all things he had said before, lines he knew by heart.

We ended up at a restaurant, the kind that had valets in red jackets and white Christmas lights in the trees.

"Not too shabby, eh?" my father said. He threw his arm around me as we walked in.

"Good evening," he said to the hostess.

She smiled or winced. It was hard to tell which.

"Two for dinner," my father said.

"You have a reservation?"

"Just two."

The hostess inhaled and looked at us sympathetically, giving us a moment perhaps to brace ourselves for the bad news.

"We're fully booked," she said. "I can make you a reservation for next . . ." She paused and looked at her calendar. "Two weeks from tomorrow."

"It's her birthday," my father said, nudging me forward.

"I'm sorry," she said, looking at me.

My father nodded. "Okay," he said, pulling a twenty-dollar bill out of his wallet. "Let's try this again. Two for dinner."

The hostess stretched out her narrow arms, crossing them at the wrists. "My hands are tied," she said.

"Let's go," I whispered.

"Well," he said to the hostess. "Congratulations on ruining my daughter's birthday."

The hostess said happy birthday as we left. On our way out, my father stopped the couple going in.

"Don't waste your money here," he said. The couple smiled nervously and continued past us.

We got back in the Mustang and drove to the second restaurant, a place named for a city in Mexico. Acapulco or Puerto Vallarta maybe. My father told me he was a regular here. We would have no problem getting in.

This new hostess was friendlier, greeting us with a big "Hola!" I recognized her from school. She usually wore tight jeans and sweatshirts.

"Would it be too much to ask," my father said to her, "for my daughter and I to have your finest table?"

"They're all pretty much the same," she said. She was wearing a costume, a full skirt with a ruffled, embroidered top.

"Then that's what we'll take," my father said.

The girl looked confused.

"Whatever's fine," I said.

We were seated at one of the many empty tables and a waiter promptly arrived with chips and salsa. My father took a moment to read his name tag.

"Manny, my man," he said. "We're ready to go."

"Shoot," Manny said, removing a pen and pad from the maroon apron around his waist.

"We will start with a margarita for me, cola for the young lady." My father looked at me for confirmation and I nodded even though I would have preferred diet. When Manny had left, my father asked what I thought of the restaurant. "Scale of one to ten," he said.

"Eight?"

"You bet," he said. He looked around the restaurant for a moment before turning to me.

"Remember when we went to Disneyland?" he asked.

I had seen the Polaroid pictures, milky from age, so we all looked like ghosts. In one photo, my father is holding me on his hip as we stand next to Donald Duck. I have Mickey Mouse ears on my head and a Band-Aid on my pudgy knee.

"Not really," I said.

We sat there for a while in the quiet restaurant, neither of us speaking until Manny arrived with our drinks.

"*Muchas gracias*," my father said, raising his glass slightly off the table, making an effort at some enthusiasm. Some joy.

"Tequila," he said to me, "is an upper. The only liquor that is. Don't forget that."

He took a sip and made a face. "Manny," he yelled. "Taste this drink," he said, holding out the glass.

"What's the problem?" Manny asked.

"Go on, buddy. Taste it."

"I can't do that, sir."

"Okay, Manny. I'll tell you what the problem is. I've got a margarita with orange juice in it." My father took another sip. "Yes, that's definitely it."

"Okay," Manny said, picking up the drink. "I'll bring you another."

"*Uno momento*," my father said. He told Manny he would finish his current drink and gladly take a second one on the house.

"I'll have to get my manager," Manny said.

"Fine, fine," my father said. "Just bring me another one. *Por favor.*"

As he drank his margarita, his skin turned pink and glistened like raw meat. I had never known my father to be a big drinker. But then, I had never really known him at all.

"Look at you," he said, setting his empty glass down. "When you were born, you know who you looked like?"

I shook my head. I had been a jaundiced baby, yellow with a wrinkled forehead and an almost translucent scalp, bald like an old man's.

"You looked like me. That's what everyone said. My nose and the close-set eyes. I didn't know whether to feel sorry for you or for myself."

"Gee," I said. "Thanks."

"Hey, hey," he said. "Let your old man finish. It's all biology.

Babies look like their fathers so us schmoes don't end up abandoning them." He paused. "We schmoes?"

I shrugged.

"The good news is you outgrew it. You're a very pretty girl," he said, and I was both flattered and embarrassed. My appearance seemed like something my father should be above noticing and yet, I was secretly pleased that he had. I rarely had an excuse to look nice, but tonight I had carefully lined of my eyes in blue-black pencil and wore my hair half up.

When Manny returned with the second attempt at a margarita, my father seemed relieved.

"You've got perfect timing, *mi amigo*," he said. "Your tip just went from fifteen percent to twenty."

"Okay, *amigo*," Manny said.

My father took the new drink and raised his glass.

"A toast," he said. "May we have many more occasions like this."

He closed his eyes and drank slowly, taking a second to contemplate the taste, and then he said, "Manny, for the love of G-dash-D, can anybody here make a decent margarita? Is that too much to ask? Do I have to make it myself? Because I will. I'd be happy to."

"Sir, I can get you another drink," Manny said. His tone was flat and unfazed. I could tell he was humoring my father. He had probably dealt with worse.

"That sounds like a brilliant idea," my father said. "A tequila on the rocks. That's ice. Nothing else. Put a lime in there, though. Just for good measure."

Once it was just the two of us, my father looked at me and said, "We don't need to have the talk about how this isn't your fault—how your mom and I still love you even if we don't love each other, and so on and so forth?"

This was apparently how my father talked about things, by announcing he would not talk about them. "I get it."

"Good," he said. "Very good." He got out of his chair and stood up.

"On your feet," he said, motioning for me to stand, and when I did, he hugged me. It was as awkward as it was necessary. Even then I knew that.

At the end of dinner, my father ordered another tequila.

"I wasn't a bad father," he said after taking a sip of his drink. "Or a bad husband. I wasn't great, but I wasn't bad."

This was my chance to say something generous, something like I love you, but I was too old to be earnest and too young to be kind.

"I know," I said. He wasn't a bad father like winter isn't a bad season, like pit bulls aren't bad dogs. Everything just is what it is.

When the bill came, my father handed it to me and asked me to do the math. I left Manny more than I should have.

"To the car," my father said, wobbling a bit as he stood, gripping the table for support.

I told my father I had to use the bathroom. I'd meet him outside.

"Okay," he said, but he continued to stand there, watching me, maybe wondering if I was old enough to go to the bathroom unchaperoned. The last ten years of my life had been a blur for him. For both of us.

The bathroom was small but private. Just one for *Señors* and one for *Señoritas*. I thought about calling a taxi to take me and my drunk father back to Versailles, but I didn't want to go to Versailles. I wanted to go home. I called my mother's cell phone and listened to the phone ring four times before she picked up.

"Honey?" she said, out of breath.

"Can you come get me?" I told her I was at a Mexican restaurant on La Cienega.

"Which one?" she asked.

"I don't know."

"Where's your father?"

"Outside, I think."

"He left you," she said, as if I had been forgotten like an um-brella or a credit card.

"He's still here."

"Put him on the phone." I heard her whisper "It's my daugh-ter" to someone.

"I can't," I said.

"Why not?"

"I'm in the bathroom."

"She's in the bathroom," she whispered, and then, as if all the pieces had suddenly come together, she said, "Oh my God. Did you get your period?"

Her voice was high-pitched and girly, thinking her late-blooming daughter finally bloomed.

"No," I said. "Just come."

I stood in the single-stall restroom with the door locked and waited for my mother. Women knocked and said hello a few times before giving up. Eventually I heard a man's voice and opened the door a crack. It was Manny.

"We only got two restrooms here," he said. He wanted to know if I was smoking or doing drugs. Both sounded like good options.

"I'm waiting for my mom," I told him.

"Maybe it would be best to wait up front," he said. Manny's voice was stern but warm.

"Where's my father?" I asked.

"At the bar."

"He's not always like this," I said, hoping it was true.

Manny nodded and walked me to the door.

"You can wait here," he said, gesturing toward the chairs at the entrance.

"Thanks," I said.

"You want a soda?"

I shook my head and he looked at me, really looked at me, for a moment putting a hand on my shoulder like a coach about to give his star pitcher a pep talk.

"You gonna be okay?" he asked.

I would have started crying if I spoke, so I gave Manny two enthusiastic thumbs-up.

About ten minutes later, my mother showed up with her guru, the former salesman who was still selling something, something that people like my mother were buying. She got out of the car and told the guru she'd be just a minute. I had met him twice. He had shaken my hand both times and told me I had a nice grip.

My mother was in the same clothes she had been wearing this afternoon. Her hair had slipped into a droopy bun.

"Baby," she said, hugging me. "Are you cold? You must be freezing." She rubbed her hands along my bare arms.

I had worn a dress for my father, sleeveless with an empire waist and an eyelet trim. My mother bought it for me at the beginning of the summer. Now it was nearly fall and this was the first chance I'd had to wear it.

"I'm fine," I said.

"Where is he?" she said.

"Can we just go?"

She grabbed my wrist and pulled me along into the restaurant.

"We're not eating," my mother announced to the hostess before she could "Hola!" us.

I saw my father right away, at the bar, his back to us. My mother must have seen him too because she picked up her pace and marched right up to him.

"Excuse me," she said, poking him on the shoulder, her finger, leaving a dent in his shirt.

He turned around and smiled at first, as if this were a happy coincidence, all of us being here. A reunion. But my mother's sneering glare must have convinced him that this was not, in fact, a social call.

"I just wanted you to know your daughter is leaving," she said. She sounded smug and victorious.

"You are?" my father said to me.

I looked down and nodded.

"Your stuff?" he said.

"That's what you're worried about?" my mother said. "Her stuff."

"I'm doing the best I can," my father said, taking his time to carefully shape his mouth around each word. "What do you want from me?"

"Why don't you just order yourself another drink?" my mother said.

There was an empty glass next to my father, another half-empty one still in his hand.

"You're such a bitch," I said. I had never called my mother this before. I had thought it, but always to myself, clamping my mouth shut and repeating it in my head. *Bitch, bitch, bitch, bitch.* This time it escaped, barely more than a whisper.

"Don't talk to your mother that way," my father said.

"Sorry," I said to no one in particular. To everyone.

We left after that, my mother and I. She put her arm around me, as if to say, no hard feelings. I wriggled out from under her grip and walked a few steps behind her.

"Adios," the hostess said, smiling cheerfully.

easy for you

When our therapist suggested we try fighting in another language, Geoff and I fought over which language to fight in. French, I said. The language of love. I had taken two semesters of it in college. That was more than ten years ago now, although I still remembered how to ask about the weather and order a steak medium rare. À point, s'il vous plait.

Geoff vetoed French. He said we needed an even playing field. No head starts. As if this were a race, as if there were a winner at the end. He had retained a smattering of Hebrew from his Sunday school days, plus he could speak a little Italian, mostly curse words he had learned during a junior year abroad. It was through this process of elimination that we settled on Russian, an unpredictable language of soft and hard sounds. Our cleaning lady was Russian and if the language was anything like she was, brusque but not unfriendly, it would be useful for arguing, for saying what we really meant.

Our first Russian lesson was on a Saturday morning. Geoff sang in the shower, while I lay on the couch in Geoff's blue chambray boxers and an old T-shirt, the words "IN TRAINING" printed on the front and "Los Angeles Marathon" on the back. I never actually ran the marathon. Sunday practice runs started at seven in the morning. I made it to the first one and slept through the rest. The fact that I still dared to wear the shirt was constant fodder for Geoff.

"How was the marathon?" he liked to tease me. "What was your time?" He had finished three marathons, all in less than four hours.

As Geoff belted the chorus to Deep Purple's "Smoke on the Water"—this was also his ringtone—I stared out the window and waited for our tutor. We had hired our cleaning lady's daughter, who arrived on time at eleven. Her body was soft like a baby's, no elbows or knees or ankles, only skin giving way to skin.

I got off the couch and attempted cheeriness as I greeted her at the door. "You must be Anna," I said, offering my left hand, the right one already preoccupied with a Bloody Mary. It was my Saturday morning ritual. My Sunday one too.

"Yes," she said, firmly shaking my hand. Anna was nineteen with clear skin and full cheeks. When her face was at rest, her bright lips remained slightly parted, giving her a perpetual look of thoughtfulness.

She looked around, carefully taking in the living room that had been decorated by a stranger, a woman Geoff had hired to order expensive smoking chairs from Paris and handcrafted pillows from Argentina.

"Your home is beautiful," she said.

"It's not really mine," I said, surprised that I'd said it even though it was how I often felt, like a guest in my own home, cleaning up after myself, careful to put everything back in its place just as I had found it. It had been about three years since I married Geoff and moved into his two-bedroom house in Beachwood Canyon, the Hollywood sign perched above us, a constant reminder of where we were. Geoff grew up here in Los Angeles and had never left. When we first met at a bar on Sunset, I told him I was from Delaware, which made me seem as exotic as our furniture. No one was from Delaware.

"So," Anna said. "What do you want to learn how to say?" She had an accent that was subtle, just enough to soften the sharpness of her words, to make them smooth and round in her mouth.

"This was our therapist's idea," I said, explaining that he had told us we needed to put down our defenses, to say the things we avoided in our native tongue.

Anna nodded. " 'I love you' is easy. In Russian, it's nothing." She batted her hand as if shooing away a fly.

"Easy for you," I said.

"Ya lyublu vas."

"Yellow blue vase," I repeated, mimicking the sounds and rhythms of her voice. Anna smiled.

"See," she said. "Easy as cake. What else?"

"I'm pregnant," I said softly. It was the first time I had spoken the words.

"You want to know how to say this?"

"Yes."

Again, I repeated the words after her, saying them over and over, until Geoff emerged from the bathroom, freshly showered and shaved, smelling of leather and cedar and Listerine.

I turned to him and stumbled through the sentence. *"Ya bere-menna."*

"You guys started without me," he said. He had on his favorite jeans, his True Religions. Not to be confused with Citizens of Humanity. When did all the denim brands start sounding like Christian ministries?

He introduced himself to Anna and said, "You've already met my wife. She's fluent in vodka."

"Ha," I said. Ha. Ha. Ha.

"But I love her regardless." He mussed my hair as if I were a child.

Geoff got to be the funny one in our relationship. I used to be funny, but after we became a couple, it seemed as if we divvied up the personality traits; he got outgoing, I got reserved; he got confident, I got needy; he got stable, I got unhinged.

I don't blame Geoff. It was not his fault that things happened this way. For two years, he had been a good boyfriend and I had been a good girlfriend. I went out to dinner with his childhood friends and his most important clients. I was clever and charming. I wore pearls and made conversation about the Getty Museum and the weather. I was grateful for white gold bracelets, diamond earrings, a Cartier watch, and finally, a ring.

After we got married, I quit my job and changed my name and my religion—I was a lapsed Catholic anyway, and I had worked in PR, which was the modern-day flight attendant. You looked pretty and kept people happy and hoped someone married you before you became an old flight attendant—or old publicist.

I had made less than thirty thousand dollars a year in my job, which was about what Geoff paid for me to join his sports club. Not that I ever used it. Instead, I spent my days walking up and down the hills of our neighborhood, getting as lost as I could, wondering what I would do if I couldn't find my way home, imagining a trail of bread crumbs to lead me back. At night, Geoff got into bed and we had the don't-touch-me-I'm-fat argument, sometimes referred to as the don't-touch-me-I'm-tired argument. "What can I do?" he would ask. "You can leave me alone," I would say.

We exhausted the next hour of our Russian lesson sitting around the dining room table and repeating the words Anna spoke, trying to replicate the way her tongue flicked against the roof of her mouth so the sounds came out choppy and neat. In Russian we learned how to say *yes, no, maybe. Hello, bye for now, till we meet again! How are things? Very well, thanks, and you? So-so, not too bad. I don't understand. Do you understand? You are beautiful, you are wise, you are kind, have a comfortable journey.*

That night Geoff called me his little babushka. He pulled me toward him and rubbed his hands over my skin, touching me in a way that felt proprietary, handling me with care, gentle but unremitting.

I knew that if I had this baby, I would belong to Geoff forever. For eternity. I would be the mother of his child.

"Babushka," Geoff said to me again, nuzzling my neck, his breath hot against my skin.

"Perogi," I said back to him as though it were a term of endearment.

"Borscht," he said.

"Vodka."

"Bolshevik," he said.

"You win." I rolled over, claiming a swath of covers.

"Come on," Geoff said. "Don't quit."

"Why not?" My back was still turned to him.

"Because it's no fun."

"I hadn't realized this was fun," I said.

"Bratwurst," he said, leaning in and whispering the word.

"That's German," I said, pulling away from him. "Game over."

I woke up on Wednesday and it was still raining. It had been for days. It wasn't supposed to rain this much. Not here. The city couldn't cope. Houses were crumbling, losing their foundations, sliding down hills.

I stayed in bed until Anna's mother arrived. Today was cleaning day. Irina would change our sheets and scrub our toilets. As she cleaned, I made pathetic attempts to help her, to be her apprentice. I rinsed the dishes, bowls with hardened bits of Cheerios clinging to them like barnacles. I took the clothes and linens out of the dryer and began to fold them. But socks were always missing, and the sheets were too big and unwieldy for me to manage. Irina clapped her hands when she saw what I was doing.

"Enough," she said. "I'm a professional here." She shook out the sheet, which rose with a quick snap of her wrists and then floated down slowly.

"So?" she said to me, pulling the sheet to her boxy chest. "How is Anna? Very smart like I tell you?"

"Yes."

"On scholarship, you know. Even her pencils and erasers, they pay for. She gets an easy ride."

I smiled. "Full ride."

Irina laughed, opening her mouth wide enough that I could see her gold molars. "Full ride," she repeated, laughing still, as if this was too much. "So," she said. "Let's hear what you learn?"

"I'm not very good."

"I'm not very good at English," she said. "Okay. Go. Say something."

"I don't think so."

"You're a poultry," she said. "A big fat poultry." She shook her head at me, exasperated.

"You're right," I said. "I am a big fat poultry."

At the last minute, Geoff had to go out of town for business. Part of me was grateful for the chance at aloneness, and yet I was still resentful of him leaving, of his freedom to come and go as he pleased.

I watched as he packed his things. I was lying on our still-unmade bed as he did a layup from the dresser and pumped his fist in the air when his boxers landed in the bag.

"You'll miss our lesson," I said, taking out the boxers, refolding them, and putting them back.

"So you'll teach me."

"I'm awful at it."

"We're both awful," he said. "That's the point."

When Anna came on Saturday, I had already finished one morning cocktail. Once I had enough to drink, my mouth could relax and the clutter of Russian consonants would flow more easily off my tongue.

"Hey," I said to her, waving from the front porch as she approached in her slow and cautious way.

"Hey," she said.

"It's just us two today."

She looked disappointed, which I guess was better than frightened.

"So, it's too nice to be indoors. Let's hang out outside," I said confidentially, as if we were in this together. It had finally stopped raining, and there was that calmness you get after a storm, when it was so quiet you could almost hear the sound of the ground gurgling.

"Do you swim?" I asked.

"Not really," Anna said.

"We have a pool."

She was still standing on the porch with her sturdy Russian legs firmly placed.

"You could borrow a bathing suit," I said.

"No thanks."

"Please," I said, pressing my palms together. "It's so nice out."

Anna looked up at the sky and squinted. "Okay," she said.

I put on a black bikini and gave Anna the only full-piece I owned, the one Geoff bought me when we went scuba diving on the Big Island. The suit was nautical, navy with white circles. It was a medium and I figured it would accommodate

Anna's shape. She was shorter than me, but fuller in the places a woman is supposed to be fuller.

"Perfect," I said when Anna stepped out of the bathroom.

The circles on the suit had stretched into ovals across her butt and hips. She was still holding her backpack, clutching it in front of her stomach. I put my arm around her and steered her downstairs to the kitchen, where I paused to make a second Bloody Mary.

"Do you want one?" I asked Anna. "Virgin, of course."

"Okay," she said.

I made one strong and another one sans alcohol, but then added a generous splash of vodka. "What the hell?" I said. "Cheers." We clinked our glasses together and Anna made a face after her first sip, her mouth turning down.

"Too strong?" I asked.

She shook her head and took another big sip, as if to prove her point. We finished one drink at the counter and then refilled our glasses before heading outside. It was still a little cool, maybe sixty-five degrees with a breeze, but it was sunny and cloudless. It seemed reassuring, a clear sky after the rain. As though everything would be okay.

Our pool, the pool that Geoff had put in, that he kept heated all year, was only five feet at the deepest end, so you couldn't dive. Not unless you were extremely careful. You had to dive out, almost parallel to the bottom. Go straight down and you'd collide with the mint green concrete.

Anna and I climbed onto the big blow-up raft, our bodies squeaking against the plastic as we adjusted our weight, distributing it evenly so we wouldn't sink or topple.

"Do you have a boyfriend?" I asked her once we were both comfortably settled, the raft drifting calmly on the water's surface.

"I did once in Russia," she said, staring up at the sky.

"Well, you're better off. Play the field." This didn't sound like something I would say. It sounded like something I heard someone else say to me once. Or maybe I stole it from a movie. Whatever it was, it made me feel old and clichéd, like a woman who had nothing left to do but reminisce, a woman who told when-I-was-your-age stories.

"Why are you trying to learn Russian? You could learn any language," Anna said. "Who wants to speak Russian? Such an ugly language."

"I wouldn't call it ugly." I explained that Geoff and I were trying to learn how to communicate, that in English, we only knew how to do two things: ignore each other and hurt each other.

"And you think it will be different in Russian?" she asked. "In Russian, you can say the meanest things." She mumbled some words I couldn't understand.

"What does that mean?"

"Your mother's a fascist pig."

"That's not so bad."

"I was being nice," Anna said.

"In vodka veritas."

"What does that mean?"

"It means you and I need another drink." I shook my glass, nearly empty now except for the melting ice and tomato juice residue.

"When did you fall out of love with your husband?" Anna asked nonchalantly, as if she was simply making conversation, asking me about my favorite band or where I went to college.

"Hobson's choice," I said.

"Who's Hobson?"

I dragged the tips of my fingers through the water and thought for a moment. "I don't know actually," I said. "But your question—any way I answer it, I lose."

Anna yawned, stretching her soft arms over her head. "It's better to lose a lover than love a loser."

"Is that a Russian saying?"

"It was on a T-shirt."

"Oh," I said. Had it really come to that? That I now clung to the wisdom of T-shirts?

Not that I thought Geoff was a loser. He definitely wasn't a loser. But the truth is that I don't know if I was ever really in love with him. I know that I had convinced myself I was. Maybe that's what you do. Maybe you decide to be in love, that you're ready for it. And by the time you realize you aren't, it's too late—you've grown attached. Your lives are intertwined; the effort of leaving becomes greater than the effort of staying.

"Did you tell him about the baby?" Anna asked. She paddled with one arm, rowing us toward the center of the pool.

"Not yet," I said, breathing in the damp air, heavy with the scent of wet leaves and dirt. I closed my eyes and put my hand over my face but I could still feel Anna looking at me, waiting for an explanation.

"What?" I said.

"Nothing."

After a few moments, Anna slid off the raft, slipping gracefully into the pool. I repositioned myself, trying to steady the raft. Anna was under for a while. I watched her through the mirrory water, her arms moving in slow circles, her hair floating around her, flickering like flames. When she came up, she exhaled loudly, water droplets spraying from her mouth.

"Is your husband back next week?" she asked, propping one arm on the raft. I told her yes, that next week it would be the three of us again. That seemed to satisfy her. I closed my eyes and let the raft drift. When I finally opened them again, Anna was out of the pool, standing by the edge and dipping her foot into the water, swinging it like a pendulum. She wobbled a bit but regained her balance.

"You okay to drive?" I asked.

"I'm Russian," she said.

I had been liberal with the vodka in her drinks, and the road, the one from our house to the bottom of the hill, was narrow and winding. You had to concentrate on keeping the asphalt under your wheels. It could be treacherous even if you were stone-cold sober. I remembered all the stories of those accidents, the ones on the six o'clock news of innocent people getting killed when they ran out to get ice cream or were on their way home from a Little League game. They were almost always close to home, almost always killed instantly.

While Anna was upstairs changing out of the bathing suit, I stopped in the kitchen for another drink. Pool water ran down my skin and left lagoon-shaped puddles on the marble floor. I shivered a bit before reaching for the vodka, Belvedere, top shelf. Only the best in this house. There was enough left for a small shot, which I took hastily, but still craved more. One drink begets another and another and another. Isn't that what they teach you in rehab?

There was a market at the bottom of the hill that sold liquor and macrobiotic sandwiches and tampons. Whatever you might need. Anna and I left together. I leaned into her as we walked out.

"Are *you* okay to drive?" she asked.

"That's my line," I said, twirling my keys around my finger.

Anna drove behind me, which, in theory, was the smart thing for her to do. Never pass a drunk driver. You're safer with them in front of you, where you can keep an eye on them. This was something my father told me back in Delaware, where everyone drove home drunk from the local T.G.I. Friday's.

My favorite part of driving was the muscle memory of it, the way my arms and feet knew how to move around a curve they knew by heart. If I thought too much about it, I might have made a mistake, might have given the car too much gas or taken the turn too sharply. Sometimes you had to trust the body, you had to stay out of its way. That's what I had been thinking about when Anna's car sailed across the wet road, hovering for a moment before slamming into mine. Immediately I put a hand to my stomach, to feel for something, anything, the swirling, eddying motion of life inside me. I sat there, afraid to move, afraid to dislodge the thing that was so narrowly tethered to my own body. After a moment, I heard Anna's voice at the door. "I'm so sorry," she was saying, her voice wobbly and blubbering. "So sorry. So, so sorry."

I didn't respond. I just kept my palm pressed to my belly, waiting for some sign, a shooting pain, a faint murmur, whatever it was that a nearly three-month-old fetus did under these circumstances.

Anna opened the door. "Does it hurt?"

"Yes," I said. It hurt. But it was a different kind of hurt, a pain that came from the absence of pain, the heavy, unbearable feeling of nothing.

Anna reached for me; she rested her hand against my shoulder and I gasped. There was something about the kindness of strangers—a condolence card from someone you barely knew, a hug from a friend you just made—that was always disarming. I felt myself crumple under Anna's touch, my body collapsing, caving in. She gently stroked my hair and whispered to me in Russian. I can't tell you a word of what she said, but I understood everything.

acknowledgments

Enormous thanks to Henry Dunow and Kate Ankofski for all their wisdom and guidance along the way.

Also, a special thanks to Denise and Brian, who both helped make this book possible.

Thanks to Rajiv and Laura, for their examples and their edits.

To Zooey, my baby. And to Neal, Mark, and Tony—muses, friends, benefactors.

Of course, deep thanks to my family: Dad, Gabby, Jordan, Todd, Hayden, Derek, Diane, Aunt Myrna, and Lisa, who might as well be family.

And to my mother: reader, writer, teacher, and all-around supporter.

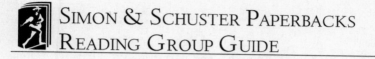

easy for you

If you've ever flown into LAX, you can picture Los Angeles from above: the undulating terra cotta roofs, translucent green swimming pools, and a maze of freeways, stretching for miles. Set within this city of actors and moviemakers, glamour and glitz, *Easy for You* depicts the universal desire to find something true.

questions for discussion

1. In "Die Meant Enough," the narrator says, "If you're alone long enough, you're bound to be someone's second something." To what extent have you seen this to be true in your own life or the lives of your friends? Do you think this is a defeatist attitude, or merely a realistic one?

2. Why do you think it's so important to the narrator to meet Dahlia, to befriend her even? Have you ever become friends with a significant other's ex?

3. Why do you think the narrator in "Swans by the Hour" is still single? Do you agree with what he seems to think—that he has not met the right woman?

4. The narrator's relationship with Ben in "Belief in Italy" could be seen as representative of the idiom "opposites attract." What do you think draws them to each other?

5. Do you think the narrator's relationship with food is better or worse by the end of the story?

6. The father in "Less Miserable" says "What's there to know?" when his son asks if Whistling Dixie is conscious of the fact that he's dying. Based on the story, do you believe that this is truly how the father feels about death?

7. Based on the character of Max Kapler in "Beverly Hills Adjacent," how do you picture the character of his wife? As a writing exercise, imagine a moment from their wedding day and share with the group.

8. In "Dog People," Erin is forced to choose Adam over Lucy. Have you ever had to give up something profoundly important to you for someone you love?

9. Imagine Erin and Adam's relationship five years from the story's end. What does it look like? Is she still friends with Paul?

10. In "Neither Here Nor There," the narrator takes note of the quote on Isabelle's wall: "The most fundamental reason one paints is in order to see." Based on this, what do you think of the images that she creates? Are they real or something in her mind?

11. The Rancho La Brea Tar Pits are very much a character in "The Last Ice Age." What neighborhood landmarks are their own characters in your town, and how do you imagine these places or structures affecting the locals as opposed to people experiencing them for the first time?

12. Do you think the narrator in "The Last Ice Age" has made any decisions she would take back? Have you ever made any decisions that you're not proud of but would make again?

13. As either a writing exercise or a conversation starter, envision a scene from "Versailles" from Manny's perspective.

14. If the narrator in "Versailles" was forced to choose one parent to live with, which one do you think she would choose? Which one would you choose for her?

15. In the collection's eponymous story, the main characters are learning Russian to better communicate. If a therapist suggested this to you and your significant other, how would you react?

16. Do you feel sympathetic for the narrator of "Easy for You," or do you think she's running from responsibility or reality when she says of being in love that "by the time you realize you aren't, it's too late—you've grown attached"?

17. One theme of this collection is the interconnectedness of an incredibly metropolitan place like Los Angeles. Were there any characters you felt would relate particularly well to one another? If you had to envision the city from above, who would you picture as neighbors? Enemies? Best friends?

enhance your book club

For your book club discussion, have a computer nearby for easy access to websites related to the city of Los Angeles. Using tourism and recreation information, construct a typical day for the main character of each story. Which photos of the city would each be drawn to, and what parts of the city would each prefer?

Have each member of your book club construct a short story about the character in their own neighborhood that they're most drawn to; it doesn't have to be the most distinctive personality but instead could be the person they've always seen and never talked to, or the quiet family next door who remain a mystery. Combine the stories into your group's own collection, and, after reading aloud, discuss what these stories say about your own city or town.

a conversation with Shannan Rouss

You no longer live in Los Angeles, yet you have chosen to set your stories there. What about L.A. is so enticing? Are there any other regions that hold the same allure for you?

I think the reason I can write about L.A. is precisely because I no longer live there. I need the distance to be able to write about it. I've lived in New York for the past nine years and have never written anything set here. When you're too close to something, it's very hard to see it clearly. And what you do see can become its own impediment.

I also spent eight years in Baltimore and occasionally I'll have a character from that part of the country but I'm not drawn to it in the way that I'm drawn to L.A. What I love so much about the city is that it truly holds its own as a character. It can be harsh and cruel, or glamorous and seductive, or completely suburban and mundane. It can be contemporary or prehistoric, the ocean or the desert. It is a city that resists being defined. That, for me, is its magic.

How much of yourself (if any) do you put into your stories?

Writers are supposed to hate this question about how much of their characters is based on their own experience. But it's inevitable, both the asking of the question and the intrusion of your own experience on your writing. I say intrusion because it often feels like that. Sometimes when I'm writing I need to take a moment to think about my character, to picture her as someone completely different from myself, in order to continue telling the story. I often steal details from my own life, but the stories and the characters have to exist separately from me. If I abided by my own narrative it would be terribly boring for the reader.

You frequently write from a man's perspective. Is this more of a challenge than writing female narrators?

Yes and no. Writing from a man's perspective allows me to get out of my own way. Assuming a male voice gives me a lot more room to invent. Of course, it also creates room for error. Fortunately I have male readers who can point out places where I may have gotten things wrong. For example, in "Swans by the Hour," the narrator initially said that he told penis jokes. A friend and reader informed me that guy would never say "penis jokes." So now it's "dick jokes."

Did any of the characters in this collection resonate with you in a particularly strong way after you were finished writing?

Answering this question feels a little bit like naming a favorite child as a mother. (Not that I'm a mother.) All the characters resonate with me, otherwise I couldn't have written their stories. That said, I would probably have to say that the character who continues to keep me up at night is Max Kapler. As much of a curmudgeon as he is, I still want to hear his voice. I can't help but hear his voice. He has so much to say, perhaps because he is the least filtered of all my characters.

"Neither Here Nor There" suggests the existence of the supernatural. Have you had any uncanny personal experiences that lead you to create this undertone?

I think as a writer you have to believe in things you can't see or know. So, do I believe in ghosts? I believe in the possibility of them. I actually love what the father in "Less Miserable" espouses, that "even with all the synapses and cells and neurons, there's nothing to explain what makes any of us alive or dead." I think that's the underpinning of "Neither Here Nor There." It's about allowing for the mystery of life and death.

In many of your stories, your characters are struggling with love,

finding it, keeping it, letting go of it. How do you think the setting of Los Angeles affects these struggles?

In L.A., it's impossible to avoid the fantasy, even if you've grown up there, even if you think you're immune to it. Maybe that's true of wherever you live to an extent. But it seems that the glamour and romance of Los Angeles promises being swept off your feet and some sort of happy celluloid ending. Certainly the narrators in "The Last Ice Age" and "Easy For You" have fallen victim to this. Oh, and the narrator in "Swans by the Hour" may be the best example by far of someone more in love with fantasy than reality.

I'd say that the foil to them might be Erin from "Dog People." It might seem as though she has settled, admitting that Adam is imperfect. But I think her choice to be with him comes from a place of strength, not weakness. There's a little bit of me in Masha when she looks at Erin's life and says, "I don't know if I could do it." I think I admire Erin for understanding that life is messy and for knowing that you have to make sacrifices, but I too don't know if I could do it.

What is your writing regime like? Do you outline first or just go where the story takes you?

Most of my ideas for short stories start from something very small—an anecdote I may have heard, an article I may have read, a person I may have observed. For example, "The Last Ice Age" began with a group of girls I saw at the airport. There was clearly a leader among the girls, the one whom the others followed, mimicking her gestures in an admiring way. And for some reason, this girl, who eventually became Reagan, both intrigued and angered me. I actually felt hostile toward her, a fifteen-year-old I didn't even know. It was this reaction that I came to explore in "The Last Ice Age."

The nice thing about writing a short story verses a novel is that you can begin with a tiny nugget, a thought, a scene, a character and just sort of write your way through it, letting your mind take its course. (In fact, I hold fast to a quote similar to the quote on Isabelle's wall—"The most fundamental reason one paints is in order to see"—from E.M. Forster: "How can I know what I think until I see what I say?") Writing is how I often find the story. And then small details, lines, and images might come to me while I'm walking my dog or trying to fall asleep. Little by little, the story comes together, through an accumulation of details and the occasional cutting of them.

With a novel, I imagine it's more difficult to do this, to simply allow the narrative to take shape, which may explain why I've only written the beginnings of novels. While I think writing a novel should still happen organically, I imagine that you need to have a firmer grasp on your starting place—even just a character—to avoid too many wrong turns. Finishing a ten-page story and then realizing you need to rewrite much of it is one thing. Finishing a two-hundred-page novel and realizing the same thing is quite another.

What are you working on now? Do you have plans to write another book?
Ah, a novel, of course. Writing short stories feels a bit like a romance, a whirlwind affair that may last a couple weeks, a month, even a few months. Of course, they linger long after they've ended, but you get to move on, entertain yourself with a new pursuit so that you can never become too bored or frustrated or lonely.

A novel on the other hand feels like so much more of a commitment, which is both terrifying and reassuring, the opportunity to spend an unforeseen amount of time in whatever world you create.

What I'm working on is set in L.A., but it's a more extreme, almost surreal vision of the city than what's depicted in these stories. I don't want to say much more than that except that it's about identity and reinvention, or "recasting" as it's called in the novel.